Lord of Eternity

Richard E. Ford

Lord of Eternity

✦

Divine Order and the Great Pyramid

Richard Ford

iUniverse, Inc.
New York Bloomington

Lord of Eternity
Divine Order and the Great Pyramid

iUniverse books may be ordered through booksellers or by contacting:

iUniverse
1663 Liberty Drive
Bloomington, IN 47403
www.iuniverse.com
1-800-Authors (1-800-288-4677)

ISBN: 978-0-595-49049-3 (pbk)
ISBN: 978-0-595-60947-5 (ebk)
ISBN: 978-0-595-49039-4 (cloth)

Printed in the United States of America

iUniverse rev. date: 11/21/08

To the three muses in my life–my grandmother whose gifts I inherited, my mother who inspired me, and my wife who listened and believed.

Contents

Illustrations

TABLES

APPENDICIES

Illustration Credits

Line drawing #3, Example of *Djed* Column. Reprinted from, R.T.
Rundle Clark, <u>Myth and Symbol in Ancient Egypt</u>, with permission of
Thames and Hudson, Ltd.

Acknowledgements

I would like to thank my family and friends–especially my wife, Annette, my brother, Patrick, and my friend and colleague Mike Omer–for their unceasing support, without which *Lord of Eternity* would have never been much more than a dream. Whenever I grew weary of the effort or discouraged, they were always there.

To Karen Davis, my patient and understanding editor, and to Drew Kraus of VideoComm Technologies, the technician and artist who assisted in creating the many indispensable graphics in *Lord of Eternity*, thank you. Your professionalism and the time and attention you gave me were invaluable. It was a pleasure working with you!

And how do I begin to thank those scholars and authors that taught me so much and without whose knowledge and insight my journey would have been all but impossible? Peter Tompkins and his seminal work, *Secrets of the Great Pyramid* and the appended compilation of Livio Catullo Stecchini's unpublished monographs, *Notes on the Relation of Ancient Measures to the Great Pyramid*, Mark Lehner, *The Complete Pyramids*, Toby Wilkinson, *Early Dynastic Egypt*, R.T Rundle Clark, Myth and *Symbol in Ancient Egypt*, Kurt Mendelssohn, *The Riddle of the Pyramids*, Adolph Erman, *Life in Ancient Egypt*, John Anthony West, *The Traveler's Key to Ancient Egypt*, Graham Hancock, *Fingerprints of the Gods*, Plato, *Timaeus*, Herodotus, *The History*, and to many others that time and space considerations won't allow for specific mention.

I am deeply indebted to all of them and I can think of no greater recognition than to echo those same sentiments spoken by Peter Tompkins in his Acknowledgements, "This is indeed a cumulative effort, and I hope that my successors in pyramidal quests will be as lively and entertaining as have been my predecessors."

Thank you!

Introduction

This may be a challenging book for some people to read; it contains a great deal of factual material of a technical nature that could be intimidating for them. Though the storyline is fictional, straightforward and uncomplicated, its principal purpose is to pace the presentation of the factual material and provide appropriate opportunities for reflection. It does not contain any thrills, or dramatic twists and turns of plot. I chose to use this creative nonfiction format, rather than making the book a work of nonfiction, in order to make the factual material as accessible as possible for people who might have an interest in the book's subject matter, but who might struggle with technical issues. Yet, it will still be difficult for them—acquiring knowledge always is.

The language of the Great Pyramid is mathematics—geometry, trigonometry, astronomy, geography, etc.—a transcendental universal language. This was by design. The people who conceived of and built the Great Pyramid knew that only the language of mathematics would endure for the ages and speak to all men in precisely the same manner, its message the same for all no matter their circumstances of time and place. It is also the language of the cosmos and gives rise to the order of all things under creation, the divine order of the universe, without which life would not be possible.

The book is not long, but it will be an arduous climb. Take your time, be patient. The factual matter gradually builds on itself. Pay especially close attention to the graphics, and take the time to stop and review each one carefully. All of them contain a wealth of information that is critical to a more complete understanding of the text. Some of them supplement and reinforce the text, while others contain material that words simply cannot do justice by. All of them, however, are an essential part of the book.

The book also contains a significant amount of speculation in order to give context where there is little to none to be had, because of the almost total lack of records from the times that the book speaks of, most of which are of the remotest antiquity. Some of the speculation is historical, some of it religious, and some of it scientific, but all of it is provided in an effort to bridge the broad gaps in the records. Otherwise, the technical material in the book would stand in an isolated silence, largely bereft of context, making its purpose and meaning very difficult to assess. This is another reason that I chose to use a creative nonfiction format to present this material.

Good luck with your read! If you persevere, you will discover the truths behind some of the greatest legends of the ages. And you will learn some of the most valued knowledge of a great civilization—knowledge that has long been suspected to exist, but which has remained hidden for thousands of years. It will be well worth all of your efforts.

Some final thoughts before you begin your journey. The Great Pyramid was profoundly sacred to the people who created it, and as a work of religious expression and belief, it is almost unparalleled in human history. While much of the material in this book is technical in nature, it is also deeply religious as well—it could hardly be otherwise in view of its subject matter. In this light, then, I can think of no more appropriate words to leave you with than those of Plato's Timaeus:

"All men, Socrates, who have any degree of right feeling, at the beginning of every enterprise, whether small or great, always call upon God."

1

The Quest

How could I possibly have known, years ago when I first set out, that such a simple quest would lead me to such a pass?

A graduate student, I hadn't chosen the subject for my doctoral thesis with any particular care or insight—nor, sad to say, with any real thought as to what I might eventually learn. Yet here I am now, utterly bewildered by that knowledge and profoundly humbled by it.

The subject was simple, almost sterile in an academic sense: "The Legends of the Great Pyramid's Connection to the Flood Myth: An Inquiry into Their Origins, and Theological and Cultural Context." I could dissect and parse out the topic at my discretion to determine when, where, and how the legends began and who started them. Straightforward enough, on the face of it. Though a little too narrow, probably with sparse source material—my academic advisor's precise comment before she reluctantly signed on to it.

But it suited me just fine at the time. Such was the unrelieved naivety of my existence. I had no feel for the prospects of success or concern for the consequences of misjudgment. I was living on family trust money, so what did it matter? If it all came to naught and I had to start over, well, so be it. Regretfully, those were my thoughts. I guess I was either serious but not fully committed or committed but not really serious. Most likely both were accurate when I began the project. Nevertheless I fully believed I would find what I was looking for and had every expectation of success.

The ancient Egyptians had enthralled me since early childhood, when my mother first mentioned them to me, and that fascination carried over into my academic pursuits. Everything about them excited my interest and curiosity and I read about them voraciously. Most of all, I devoured everything I could find on the Great Pyramid (a side profile of the eastern

1

aspect and principal interior spaces are depicted in Appendix 1). To me, as to most people, it embodies their civilization, invoking all of their mysterious ways and beliefs. I never cease to be awed by it. In the several instances when I have been privileged to stand before it, I am not ashamed to admit that I look up at its staggering immensity in openmouthed, childlike wonder. A mountain reared by the hand of man, built to a standard of perfection that defies belief. Endless superlatives have been used to describe it, but my thoughts always end the same way: surely its builders had God uppermost in mind. This was the genesis of my thesis selection.

Interpretations about the purpose of the Pyramid, which is how I will hereafter refer to it, fall into two camps: (1) It was designed and built as a tomb for Pharaoh Khufu. (2) It embodies in its dimensions a vast ledger in stone of geographic and geometric measures and formulas and was never intended to serve as a mere tomb. These interpretations have engendered constant and endless argument, and neither camp is predisposed to seek common ground with the other.

Certainly Khufu could have used it as his final resting place and certainly it could have been built to preserve certain mathematical and geometric principles, including the transcendental factors π (pi) and φ (phi). Both camps may in fact be correct, but both miss the point. To me the Pyramid's purpose must reflect more than these two opposing, pedestrian views. The Pyramid-as-tomb interpretation tends to discourage further lines of inquiry, while the Pyramid-as-ledger-of-knowledge interpretation can become mired in arcane detail. Both interpretations lose sight of the larger purpose of the Pyramid: that it must have been a profound statement of religious belief made before both God and man, rendered to endure for eternity. My desire to find the exact nature of this statement led me to inquire into the legends connecting the Pyramid with the Flood myth. I thought something in these legends might shed light on this larger statement. This possibility energized and guided my quest.

Jewish and Arabic writers supposedly authored the simple, straightforward legends during the Middle Ages. Although the accounts varied somewhat, all stated that the Pyramid was built to preserve the accumulated knowledge of mankind in the face of an impending catastrophe, which would result in the great Flood and the almost total destruction of the Earth. The knowledge supposedly hidden away in the Pyramid consisted of astronomical and geometrical knowledge, machines, and terrestrial globes and celestial spheres. Some writers said that the Pyramid also contained accurate charts of the stars, as they appeared many thousands of years ago. Some implied that the date of the catastrophe was recorded. Ebn Wasuff Shah stated that men had foreseen that the catastrophe would occur when "the Heart of the Lion would reach the first minute of the Head of Cancer." Abu Zeyd el Balkhy stated that the Pyramid was built when the "Lyre was in Cancer," just before the catastrophe.

That pretty much summed up the legends and I was determined to find what gave rise to them and whether any of them were rooted in fact. Or were they all simply fiction, as informed academic opinion has long believed? I was curious also whether the legends began as tales the Egyptians handed down or were instead fanciful inventions of the Jews and Arabs, based wholly on their own traditions and myths.

I promise that you will not be disappointed to learn what I discovered.

You will also learn that the title of this work holds the most profound meaning imaginable. If the Pyramid had a name it would be Lord of Eternity, for not only does that invoke the deepest-held religious beliefs of ancient Egypt, it also is a timeless connection to God and Heaven. No title is more appropriate.

I have said that my quest was what eventually led me to uncover revelations regarding the Pyramid. That is not entirely accurate. I pursued my thesis for several years in various libraries, including several in Egypt, to no avail. I read endless manuscripts and books that all led nowhere. My thesis had little to support it and I reluctantly came to that realization, but I couldn't bear to just end it with so little to show for my efforts. I decided to visit the Pyramid one final time to try to find some inspiration and reason to continue. A long shot, for sure! And it was during idle conversation with a fellow passenger in the airport, while on my way to Egypt that I first learned of Hordadef.

In retrospect, the gentleman's remarks hardly did Hordadef justice, but at the time I took from our conversation the thought that this Hordadef was an interesting character who told interesting stories. Little more than that. How could he be more? How could a cab driver possibly have knowledge that had eluded scholars for centuries? Still, it was his name that intrigued and stuck with me.

When I got to my hotel in Egypt I asked about him, hoping that he would enliven my visit if nothing else, and maybe lift my spirits from the gloom and sense of hopelessness that had settled over my quest. I never expected to learn anything meaningful from him. How utterly wrong I was.

What Hordadef's real name was I haven't a clue, as he never revealed anything meaningful about either his family or his background. While he invariably claimed to be a cab driver, I suspect he was much more than that. You probably will, too. But for the moment I will not say more than this, for this work is as much a story about him as it is about the Pyramid. I will say that he did not take the name of Pharaoh Khufu's brother, a priest of Egypt and one of her greatest wise men, without reason. For a purported cab driver, his connection to the Pyramid was incredible, and what I learned from him was almost beyond belief.

2

A Contract Between Men

I arrived in Egypt around midnight and spent the next hour or so claiming my bags and clearing customs and immigration. After exchanging dollars for Egyptian pounds, I hailed a cab to the Mena House Hotel, at the foot of the Giza Plateau below the Great Pyramid. The hotel was not inexpensive but there was none better located for visiting the pyramids, so the added cost was well worth it. By the time I checked in and found my room, I was exhausted and ready for sleep.

I awoke late that morning . . . later than I wanted to. I'd scheduled an appointment with the Egyptian Antiquities Authority to see whether I could gain access to those parts of the Pyramid not open to the public, such as the subterranean chamber and Davidson's chamber. I carried a letter of introduction from the head of my university's Department of Oriental Studies, which I hoped would get me the permission I needed.

After a quick breakfast I sought out the hotel concierge, who asked if I needed a cab. I said yes, but then remembered that I wanted to meet Hordadef and told him I had already arranged for one. I thanked him anyhow.

When I stepped out of the hotel the winter air was cool but not uncomfortable. I glanced up at the Pyramid as a host of cab drivers descended on me, offering their services. I shouted at large whether anyone knew Hordadef, and a man to one side hollered back, "Who asks for Hordadef?"

The owner of the voice was clean-shaven, middle-aged, and dressed in a faded print shirt and jeans a little too snug for his mid section. He smelled distinctively of tobacco and aftershave. As he stepped forward, he smiled broadly and thrust out his hand. I took it.

"I am Hordadef," he said proudly. "And who is this that I have the pleasure of meeting?"

"Richard Camden. Call me Richard."

"Ah, Mr. Richard, welcome, sir. Welcome to Egypt! May your stay with us be most enjoyable, most enjoyable, indeed. And how is it that I might be of service to you today, Mr. Richard?"

"I have an appointment at the Antiquities Authority at half past eleven."

"The Antiquities Service, of course. Yes indeed. Please, Mr. Richard, step this way." He guided me across the street and into the back seat of an aging blue car of uncertain make or model. As we pulled away from the curb, he leaned out the window and yelled something in Arabic to the other drivers, who laughed as we sped away.

"Is this your first visit to Egypt, sir?"

"No, I have been here five or six times now."

"Then you know a little of this Egypt, no?"

"Yes, it is a fascinating land," I responded almost reflexively, while absent-mindedly staring out the window. The oppressiveness of my fruitless quest overtook me again, darkening my mood.

"That it is, indeed it is! And what do you find most fascinating about it?"

"Oh, I guess I would have to say the pyramids."

"The pyramids, yes! And do you know a lot about the pyramids?"

Before I could answer, the car braked suddenly for a bicycle that swerved in front of us and Hordadef leaned on the horn for over a minute. Then he jerked his steering wheel left and went around the bicyclist, but in doing so cut off the driver behind us, who leaned on his horn. Hordadef swerved again to the left, ostensibly to change lanes. But keeping orderly lanes is foreign to Egyptian drivers, who recognize no such boundaries. I thought the street had six lanes, three in each direction, but it was hard to tell. Cars constantly jockeyed for position. Buses, trucks, and the occasional donkey-drawn cart added to the chaos, as did the constantly blaring horns. I saw traffic lights, but no one took them completely seriously—some cars stopped, others didn't.

As I watched the traffic buffeting us from all sides, I thought, *How is it that the Egyptians of old could find the discipline and organization to raise the pyramids, while their descendants can't manage simple traffic?*

"Do you know a lot about them?" Hordadef asked again.

"Yes, of course. I majored in Ancient Egyptian Civilization and studied them quite extensively. I've also visited them a number of times during my several trips to Egypt."

Hordadef let out a low whistle. "You must truly be an expert, then. And no doubt you must have some big meeting with the Antiquities people to discuss some very important things about them, no?"

"Yes…I mean, no. Actually, I'm just looking to get their permission to explore some areas inside the Great Pyramid. I'm doing research on it and I'm hoping to find some things that may help me understand why it was built."

"I am impressed, Mr. Richard, and I know you are only being modest with me. You must be an expert, with all of your education. And here we are. The Antiquities Service, Mr. Richard." He swung the cab into an angled parking slot in front of a massive government building. "I'll wait for you."

"How much will that cost me?"

"It's all included in the daily fare."

"The daily fare? I never agreed to a daily fare! How much is it, anyhow?"

"It is £200, or $65, plus tip."

"That's ridiculous! How much for this trip?"

"Trip's included, Mr. Richard. I only work on daily fare."

"But I never agreed to the daily fare!"

"Excuse me, excuse me, Mr. Richard, but it was you who called for Hordadef, was it not? Hordadef did not call for Mr. Richard and Hordadef only works at the daily rate."

"I'm already late. I can't talk about this now. We'll discuss it later."

I jumped out of the cab and strode into the building. I guess I should have known that the time of my appointment wouldn't matter. I waited over an hour before Mrs. Alawi appeared in the lobby to motion me into her office.

After a few pleasantries, I told her the purpose of my visit and passed her my letter of introduction. She looked briefly at the letter and handed it back to me. She was sorry, but the Authority wouldn't be able to honor the request at that time due to other commitments and higher priorities. We discussed the issue for about ten minutes before I was convinced that she either couldn't or wouldn't give me permission.

She did, however, give me the name of a tourist guard at the pyramids who could schedule me for an after-hours visit for $500 an hour. This would allow me to see most areas of the Pyramid, but not the chambers above the King's Chamber. I protested that that was not satisfactory, but she raised her hand and said that was all that was possible for the moment. I asked to speak to her supervisor, but she said that he was out of the country. I was frustrated and quite angry, but it was readily apparent that there was nothing more I could say or do to change her mind. I looked at her for several seconds in silence while she gazed down at some paperwork in front of her. She then looked up at me without saying a word. I rose and thanked her for her time and departed the office.

I was in a really foul mood. I began to feel that not only was my thesis a bust but I was apparently just wasting my time in returning to Egypt.

Hordadef was standing on the sidewalk, leaning against his cab.

"Okay, let's go."

"Certainly, Mr. Richard." He ushered me into the back seat. As he entered the car he turned and asked, "Where are we going now, Mr. Richard?"

"Back to the hotel," I said sullenly, with a tinge of anger.

"So, did you get the permission you were looking for?"

"No, but she gave me the name of a guard who would let me into the pyramids after hours, for $500 an hour."

"Who told you that?"

"Mrs. Alawi."

"Mrs. Kadisha Alawi?"

"Yes, that's her."

"She is a thief, Mr. Richard. She's in cahoots with the guards."

"She's a thief? She's a thief, Hordadef?" I was bewildered. "So what are you but a thief yourself?"

"Excuse me, Mr. Richard, excuse me, but I am a businessman, providing a service. Your Mrs. Alawi provides no service, yet she will take a cut of whatever you pay this guard for recommending you to him. That is what thieves do. If you want to spend an hour in the Pyramid, I can get you in for $200 an hour, but it may not be tonight. We'll have to make an appointment."

"So, you'll get a cut of the fee, instead of Mrs. Alawi. What's the difference to me?"

"Ah, Mr. Richard, you are angry for nothing. Let us go see the Pyramid and maybe that will make you forget Mrs. Alawi."

"Yes, and maybe you can tell some of these stories of yours, too, that you're supposed to be so famous for," I replied sharply.

"Why don't you tell me what you're looking for and maybe I can help you."

"You? You're a cab driver. What could you possibly know about the Pyramid that isn't already common knowledge?"

"You might be surprised at what I know. Why don't you tell me what you're looking for and maybe I can help you find it."

I wanted to drop the whole subject, but my lingering anger from the morning's disappointments ebbed away. "Supposedly there is a connection between the Great Pyramid and the story of the great Flood. Also, there are legends from Arab and Jewish writers from the Middle Ages that some antediluvian king hid all of the accumulated knowledge of his age in the Pyramid in order to preserve it from the Flood, including certain machines, terrestrial globes, celestial spheres, and star charts as they appeared at the time, as well as malleable glass. That's what I'm looking for, the truth behind these legends. It is the reason I came to Egypt."

"Well, the machines, or rather the remains of them, and the terrestrial globes and celestial spheres are all still there. Star charts, too. But I believe the malleable glass may be missing. I don't know for certain, though. I'll have to look into that one."

I was dumfounded. Could he really be familiar with the very subject I was researching? Surely he was humoring me. Still, maybe he knew something that could prove useful.

"Of course," Hordadef continued, "if you want me to show you these things, there are fees for my services, and we will have to negotiate and agree on a contract. I do not work for free. However, maybe we should go to the Pyramid tonight and I will tell you some of my so-called stories. If you are not satisfied, you will owe me nothing and we will go our separate ways, you and I. On the other hand, if you are satisfied, we will negotiate, man to man, what I am to be paid. Is that fair enough, Mr. Richard?"

Minutes later the cab pulled up in front of the hotel. Hordadef turned and looked directly at me.

"Yes, that sounds fair. I'm still a little tired from the trip, and I'd like to take a nap and get something to eat. So a night visit sounds perfect. Say seven o'clock?"

"Yes, Mr. Richard, that will be fine. Now about my fare for today . . ."

"Yes, Hordadef. Will $75 be enough?"

"As you say, Mr. Richard, as you say." He reached over the seat to accept the money, smiling broadly. "And I promise you, you will not be disappointed tonight. Seven o'clock, then. You and I will visit the Pyramid and talk of Egypt's sacred things."

Again he left me speechless. Why would a cab driver view the Pyramid as a sacred thing? But I dismissed the thought, overwhelmed by the morning's events and the disappointing outcome of my meeting with Mrs. Alawi. I needed to sleep.

I awoke around sunset and looked at my watch. Ten minutes to seven and I still hadn't eaten anything. I quickly dressed, wondering whether to tell Hordadef to forget the whole thing. I started to feel foolish for ever coming to Egypt, especially after having been refused an access pass by the Antiquities Authority.

I thought about Hordadef and his stories and decided that it would all undoubtedly cost a lot of time and money and produce little or nothing in the end. As I departed the room and closed the door behind me, I was convinced that I should see if I could catch an earlier flight back to the States.

I strode across the lobby to the entrance of the hotel. Yes, this was the best course of action. I would worry about the thesis later.

Dusk had settled in and a reddish hue tinged everything. Hordadef saw me coming and crossed the street from where he had parked his car to greet me.

"Mr. Richard, Mr. Richard, I hope you are feeling better now that you've rested and eaten a little."

"Yes, much better, thank you."

Before I could say anything more he opened the back door to the cab to show me in. This surprised me, as I had expected that we would walk up the plateau to the pyramids. I entered the cab, however, without question.

Hordadef said no more, jumped into the cab, and drove straight up the road to the plateau. As he passed the security checkpoint, he honked his horn and waved to the guards, who waved back. At the top of the plateau he swung the car to the right and came to a stop, some way from the Pyramid, which loomed to the side of us. Both of us exited the cab at the same time, and as we did so Hordadef loudly stated, "Magnificent, magnificent as always," as he leaned his head back and looked up at the stupendous structure. Even at a distance it did not fail to overawe. I, too, gazed up and felt the same rush of excitement. But I was silent.

"So, Mr. Richard, the stories begin tonight, no? And what a beautiful night, too!"

I hadn't noticed before but the temperature was perfect. I also had the fleeting thought that I'd changed my earlier intention to dispense with this trip with Hordadef.

* * *

"Now tell me, Mr. Richard, do you know the ways of heaven?"

"Do I know the ways of heaven? What are you talking about?"

"Heaven, Mr. Richard. Do you know the ways of heaven, or as you call it, astronomy and the motions of the Earth?"

"A little."

Hordadef stared at me for a moment. "So much education, Mr. Richard, yet so little knowledge; it is indeed a wonder. We will do what we can, then, you and I, and with God's blessings maybe He will guide me in my teachings and lead you to knowledge."

He came around the car to my side and motioned me to accompany him to a spot some distance from the car and the Pyramid.

"Now, Mr. Richard, point out to me the polar star, Polaris."

Fortunately I remembered the Big Dipper's relationship to the polar star from my scouting days as a youngster and was able to find it for him.

"Very good, Mr. Richard. Now do you observe that it marks the North celestial pole and sits directly above the north pole of the Earth, as the Earth turns on its axis, which runs between the north and south poles? And do you also observe that your arm is making about a 30° angle with the level of the ground?"

"Yes."

"Very well. Now, Mr. Richard, the celestial pole stands at 30° altitude above the horizon, because we are standing here, with the Pyramid, on the thirtieth parallel of the Earth, or at 30° north latitude. If we were to move closer to the North Pole, the celestial pole would appear to rise up in the heavens until, upon our reaching the pole, it would stand directly over our heads, at 90° north." He pointed directly above us.

"Now, Mr. Richard, point out to me the Great Seat."

I had heard this term before and thought that it applied to the North celestial pole, but I had to admit to him that I wasn't sure where it was located. He looked at me in silence for a moment, then laid his arm across my shoulder and alongside my head while pointing at the heavens to the left of Polaris. Then he slowly moved it sideways and slightly upward until he came to what appeared to be a blank spot in the heavens, where he stopped.

"That, Mr. Richard, is the Great Seat, the center of the universe, the eternal place that lies beyond all time, the North pole of the ecliptic. It is obscured in the blackness that will forever hide divine purpose from the eyes of man, until the end of days. The Egyptians called it Ptah and believed it to be the Throne of God. It is the most sacred spot in the heavens and it is the source of all order in heaven and on Earth, including all measures of time and distance. All of creation began from Ptah and is sustained by it to this day. Never forget this.

"Now Ptah, Mr. Richard, stands some 24° from the North celestial pole and appears to swing in a great circle with a radius of 24° about it. But that is only its apparent motion as a result of the motions of the rotation of the Earth. In reality, it is the North celestial pole that swings in a circle with a radius of 24° about Ptah, not the other way around. Its movement, however, is so slow as to be all but imperceptible, as it takes 25,920 years for the North celestial pole to complete a circle around Ptah. Do you understand?"

"No, not really."

"Well, you'll just have to accept that it does because the motions of the Earth make it appear to be the other way around, just as our eyes tell us that the Sun orbits the Earth, when we all know that it is exactly the opposite. For the moment, however, let us concentrate on Ptah's relative motion, what we see with our eyes, instead of actual motion.

"Do you observe, Mr. Richard, that as Ptah moves higher in the heavens each day," which he mimicked with his arm, circling around the North celestial pole until it was at an angle directly above Polaris, where he stopped his motion, "it would rise to an altitude of approximately 54° above the horizon at its maximum height, which is called its southing or superior culmination?"

"Yes, I see that."

"Good! Now this is very, very significant to everything that I am going to tell you tonight, Mr. Richard, and everything that will follow. When Ptah reaches this altitude, or moves to its maximum height in the heavens, it lies south of the North celestial pole. Are we agreed?"

"Yes."

"Very good, Mr. Richard. You are a good student, indeed! Now, do you know what right triangles are? Do you know geometry and its twin, trigonometry?"

"Not very well."

He paused to look at me again as he muttered under his breath, "So much education, so little knowledge. How are such things possible? May God have mercy.

"Okay, Mr. Richard, a right triangle is any triangle that has 90° as one of its angles." He stepped to the side, raising one arm directly over his head while holding the other one out to his side. "Do you see this right triangle?"

"Yes, I see."

"Good, now do you know the three right triangles that God used to construct the universe? The three right triangles that Plato spoke of in *Timaeus*?"

I couldn't answer him and he knew I couldn't, but instead of stopping again he went on.

"Okay, the first has angles of 30°–60°–90°, the second has angles of 45°–90°–45°, and the third has angles of 54°–36°–90°. All three can be found here at the site of the Pyramid. The 30°–60°–90° triangle forms from the location of the North celestial pole at an altitude of 30° above the horizon at this spot, the 60° angle lies at the location of the North celestial pole, and the 90° angle is formed by dropping an imaginary line directly down to the horizon from the North celestial pole.

"The 45°–90°–45° triangle forms from the fact that the Pyramid sits at the apex of the Nile delta, which makes a 45°–90°–45° triangle at this spot, while a second one of even greater significance is also formed here, but we will not speak of it tonight. There is a second 30º–60º–90º triangle, too, but we will speak of that on another occasion as well.

"Now the third triangle, 54º–36º–90º, is the most important of all. It is formed from the southing location of Ptah, at 54º altitude above the horizon at this spot, while Ptah sits at 36º, and the 90º angle is formed by dropping an imaginary line directly down to the Earth below its apparent location above the horizon."

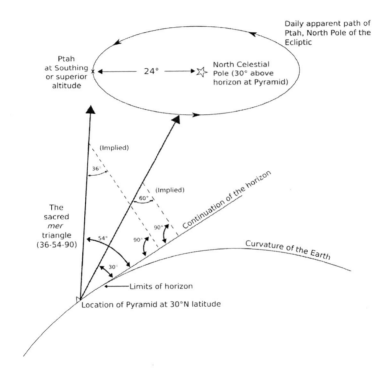

Triangles and the Pyramid's Location

Figure 1

He stopped and stared at me for a minute. He could see I was struggling to digest what he had said. He turned and pointed to the Pyramid. "You see that everything associated with the Pyramid is a triangle of one sort or another, do you not, Mr. Richard? All of the knowledge incorporated into it is preserved in triangles. That is why all of this is so important.

"Let us continue, then, with Ptah at 54° altitude and the 54°–36°–90° triangle. Here's where this all ties together for us, Mr. Richard, and it demonstrates that the Pyramid was intentionally built at this precise location because of the convergence of these three triangles here at the Pyramid's location.

"Ptah was worshipped as Ptah, South-of-His-Wall, which has confused and baffled archeologists since they began studying Egypt. But the term really just refers to the fact that Ptah reaches culminating or southing altitude here at the Pyramid at 54° altitude. Ptah in this relative location quite literally stands south of his walls, here or the walls of heaven. This location in the heavens is referred to as the Palace of the Soul of Ptah, or *Aegyptah*, which is the origin of the name Egypt.

"The 54°–36°–90° triangle was named *mr* or *mer*, which gave Egypt another name that it was known by to the ancients: *To-Mer*, or 'land of *mer*.' It is also important to our discussions to know that *Msr*, which means 'land that is divided or delineated,' is the name by which Egypt is known throughout the Arab world to this day. So you see, Mr. Richard, the Pyramid is the beginning of Egypt in a quite literal sense and it also ties the land to the Great Seat of Heaven. Once a day, as it has since time began, Ptah rises to 54° altitude in the heavens. From this spot then, quite literally, Egypt was laid out, as was the Earth itself later on. In this sense the Pyramid is the benchmark of the Earth. The Pyramid marked the prime meridian for thousands of years, until it was subsequently relocated away from Egypt after the land had settled into a period of prolonged decline."

He paused. "You look like you have a question for me."

"Yes, I do. From all of my studies I know that Ptah was a god, but only one of many Egyptian gods. He is the god of artists and craftsmen, but not the preeminent lord of the universe that you imply."

"We are both correct, Mr. Richard. Ptah is the lord of the universe, as you describe him, and he sits at the center of the universe, exactly as I have said. All of creation, all order, all life originated with him. Ptah is God; however, his role in the cosmic order of the universe became confused over the years because his great temple in Memphis was the chief learning center for artists and craftsmen. This came about because Imhotep, Egypt's Greatest of Seers and the Keeper of the Secrets of Heaven and Earth, taught there.

"Imhotep was a preeminent priest, as well as a learned astronomer, architect, mathematician, and doctor. He was also the Chief Pot Maker of the Royal Palace, which sounds like a fairly insignificant position but in fact was one of his most important. He did not work with clay but with stone, and the very hardest stones in Egypt, at that. Early in his life he learned to carve cups and vases from granite, diorite, and quartz, among others, which requires great technical skill as well as a highly developed level of artistry. He was a master at his craft, the knowledge of which he later used to build in stone on a massive scale. He didn't carve the stones for these structures himself, but trained others in this art at the Temple of Ptah in Memphis. His students grew into accomplished artists and builders in their own right, and in turn passed their skills to the young. This was how Ptah later became identified with artists and craftsmen."

He paused again to allow me an opportunity to ask further questions.

"How were the ancient Egyptians able to find and measure the apparent movements of such an inconspicuous spot in the heavens as Ptah, the North pole of the ecliptic?"

"Through long and careful observation of the North celestial pole, the Egyptians became aware that it moved slowly over time and seemed to trace out a circular path in the heavens. They measured the arc of the North celestial pole and determined the approximate location of Ptah. Then, to find its exact location, they built a structure, a device, from which they could observe this spot when it reached its lower culmination in the heavens at approximately 6° altitude from the Pyramid's location. This device was the chamber in the Pyramid known as the Queen's Chamber.

"Before the Pyramid was completed in the form that we see it today, it was used as an observatory for a long period. The Queen's Chamber was placed precisely at the level required to observe and measure Ptah at lower culmination, which the ancients could observe through the shaft that gives access to this space and that was formerly open to the sky before the Pyramid was completed, sealing it up. The niche that is found in the eastern wall of this room was used to measure their observations."

"Very interesting."

"Now, Mr. Richard, returning to our earlier subject, it is imperative that you understand that the Pyramid holds no secrets, only the preserved knowledge of Heaven and Earth. Whatever you find in the Pyramid, you will find its counterpart in the heavens and on Earth. All are the same, Mr. Richard. Are we agreed?"

"Yes," I said meekly, almost embarrassed at the thought of his speaking at levels mostly beyond me and desperately hoping he wouldn't mention my education again.

"All are the same," he repeated. "Now I am going to give you something that my father gave to me when I was a young boy, and his father gave to him, and his father to him, and so on and so on. It contains all of the knowledge that you are seeking." He handed me a small, folded piece of paper. "You will read this every night before you go to bed and on waking in the morning, and you will commit its words to memory. Do you understand? Also, you will not ask me any questions about it until we are finished with our lessons."

"Yes," I said, accepting the piece of paper from him.

"Well, then, Mr. Richard, I am satisfied that we are done for the evening, unless you wish to continue."

"No, that's quite enough for one night, Hordadef. I'm satisfied, too."

"Very well, then! You have been a very good student, Mr. Richard, and I think that things will go well for both of us. Very well indeed. Which brings us to the subject of my fee." He lit a cigarette as we spoke.

All I could do was lower my head and shake it slowly, as I smiled to myself. *What a piece of work,* I thought. *What a piece of work.* But it was he who was in control, not I, and that was what I really found disquieting. "So how much are we talking about?"

"I'm thinking $200 a day plus expenses," he said, speaking through lips clenched tightly around the cigarette in his mouth, "plus my daily rate. Oh, and my tip, too!"

"Yes, of course, the tip, too," I muttered softly. *What a piece of work.* "You know you really are a thief, don't you?"

"Excuse me, excuse me, Mr. Richard. A thief? I am a businessman offering a service," he said, pointing his right hand, which was cupped around the cigarette, toward me. "You are man and I am man, and we are talking man-to-man about a business contract for my services. A thief, Mr. Richard, takes and gives nothing in return, like the teachers at this university that you spent a fortune to attend, and yet it seems you have gained very little knowledge from them. There is thievery, Mr. Richard!"

"But I think your so-called fees are a little excessive, especially as you're including your daily cab rate on top of them."

"Excuse me, Mr. Richard, excuse me. But here you are in the middle of the deserts of Egypt, at night, arguing with a simple cab driver over the trifling sums that he asks of you to give you the knowledge that your professors failed to give, after you paid them a fortune for it. And you want to call him a thief, too. Mr. Richard, I am hurt. You hurt my heart."

"Oh, all right, agreed: $200 a day, plus expenses, plus the daily rate, plus a tip, but I'm not paying for tonight!"

"Mr. Richard, we agreed earlier that if you were dissatisfied with my services, you would not pay, and just a few moments ago you said you were satisfied."

"You're right, you're right. We did agree. Here's your $200 fee and a $20 tip."

"Ah, Mr. Richard, there is also the small matter of our $24 entry fees to the plateau and $20 *baksheesh* for the Antiquities Authority guards to permit us access to the vicinity of the Pyramid after closing hours, which I took the liberty of prepaying so that we would not be delayed. Both very legitimate expenses incurred quite legitimately."

I exhaled slowly, staring at him as I reached in my pocket. As I handed him the cash, I noticed he was smiling the whole time but not looking at me. What a piece of work. But the depth and breadth of his knowledge was beyond anything I had ever encountered. I had to admit to myself that this Hordadef was a marvel. Suddenly the thought occurred to me to ask him if it would be all right if I took notes and later told others of what he was relating to me.

"By all means, Mr. Richard, you may write everything down or tell anyone who shows an interest. It would be far better, however, if instead of notes you committed these things to memory. Memory preserves such knowledge better than anything else. Writing things down invites others who may disagree or not understand to destroy them, which destroys the knowledge. Is this not so?"

"Yes, but I do not trust my memory."

He stared back at me for a moment but said nothing further.

He drove me back to the hotel, where we said goodnight. He said we should meet around ten o'clock the next morning, to discuss what stories he would tell me next and where he would take me. He smiled and waved as he drove off.

I stood on the curb, looking after him, and smiled as I went into the hotel. *Excuse me, Mr. Richard, excuse me,* kept echoing in my mind and I thought I would laugh out loud. What a piece of work!

I showered and brushed my teeth, a little hungry but not feeling like going down to one of the restaurants. I switched off the light and climbed into bed. I was quickly lost in thought about the day's events when all of a sudden I remembered Hordadef's note. I jumped up, turned on the light, and retrieved it from the pocket of my pants. Leaning toward the lamp on the table I read:

Do you not feel the stupendous power of the Earth as it moves in measured step to the Order set for it by the Hand of God at the beginning of time?

And do you not see Earth's movements reflected in Heaven above, as cycles of time are endlessly repeated according to Divine Order for all eternity?

And do you not know that time is but the shadow of God's presence in the universe, and that He is the Lord of Eternity, the Master of Time?

Then do you not understand that the Pyramid stands between Heaven and Earth, and is a memorial to these things and a legacy to the ages?

I folded the note and put it on the table by the lamp, but almost immediately picked it up and read it again. I stood there thinking about the words for a while before turning the light off and returning to bed. Who was this Hordadef and how did he come by such knowledge?

3

The Terrestrial Globe

I awoke early. After I showered and dressed, I reread Hordadef's note several times. It was beautifully succinct and obviously filled with meaning that had escaped me the previous evening. I recalled that Hordadef had instructed me not to mention it, but my level of curiosity was such that I was determined to bring up the issue anyway.

As I closed the door to my room and walked to the elevator, it dawned on me that we had not discussed plans for the day. *A minor oversight,* I thought. As far as I was concerned, we would talk about the terrestrial globe and celestial spheres of legend and how the Pyramid was tied into the Flood myth, which was why I had traveled to Egypt. Hopefully, though, he would be able to explain these issues to me without testing the limits of my education as he had the night before.

I felt a tinge of embarrassment over my inability to grasp much of what he had told me, though I recalled having read somewhere that the location of the Pyramid was specifically chosen to act as a benchmark in delineating and laying out the land. The triangles still puzzled me, but I accepted what Hordadef told me regarding them. If he was accurate about Plato's mention of the three triangles in *Timaeus,* then they were significant, as *Timaeus* was largely based on the knowledge of the ancient Egyptians, which included geometry. In any case, it was fascinating to learn that the one triangle, 54°–36°–90°, and the location of Ptah at its southing altitude above the Pyramid were both directly related to the several names of Egypt. For the moment, this was the limit of my appreciation and understanding. I hoped it would become clearer later on.

I ordered a big breakfast to make up for missing dinner the night before and stared out the window at the lush and beautifully maintained grounds of the hotel. Birds flew in and out of the trees and bushes. As I sat admiring the scene, I shook my head at the contradiction of such life in the midst of the dry and desolate desert surrounding it. The words of the waiter, asking if I needed anything further, aroused me from my musings. I shook my head and said "No, thank you," glancing down at my watch and noting that it was ten minutes past ten. I quickly signed the check he placed beside me and left.

Outside the hotel I looked for Hordadef but couldn't see him anywhere, although his car was parked in the same location it had been the day before. I started for it when someone called after me, "Are you Mr. Richard?" I turned. One of the other cab drivers approached me. "Are you Mr. Richard, sir?"

"Yes."

"Good morning, sir. Hordadef asks that you please wait for him. He has gone up the road to talk with the Antiquities Service guards and shouldn't be more than a minute or two."

"Thank you." I turned to look up the road toward the pyramids, which dominated the landscape in that direction. I was debating whether to start up the road myself or head back into the hotel grounds to sit and wait when I heard his booming voice. "Mr. Richard, good morning, Mr. Richard. How are you today? Did you sleep well?"

"Very well, thank you."

"Good, good, that is very good! Today we have many new stories to tell, very many new stories that I am certain you will find very interesting, indeed. Come, Mr. Richard, we are heading to the Cairo Museum today." He motioned me to his cab.

"But if we're heading to the Museum, why were you talking with the guards earlier?"

"Ah, the guards, yes, well, that concerns tonight's stories." He dropped the issue as he eased me into the cab. I let it go, too. We sped away from the curb and were soon lost in the riot of Cairo traffic.

"Mr. Richard, I'm sure that a man of your obvious knowledge and experience with Egypt has been to the Museum many, many times, and Hordadef does not mean to bore you with yet one more visit. But you must see some things so that you might understand my words better. I assure you, though, all of what we will see and discuss in the Museum will be of relevance to the Pyramid."

"I'm sure it will, Hordadef, but I have some questions regarding the note that you handed me last night and asked that I read every night and every morning."

"The note, of course. But there is no need for us to discuss it now, as you will know the meaning of its words when we have finished our lessons."

I accepted his answer for the moment. Another larger question had come to mind. "You keep saying 'lessons' as if we were going to be together for quite a while. Exactly what do you have in mind, as all I'm really interested in are finding the terrestrial globe and celestial spheres in the Pyramid, which you said were still there, and learning how the Pyramid was connected to the Flood myth."

"And you will indeed learn of these things, Mr. Richard, but I must teach you other things first, so that you can understand them. All are connected, and it is hard to speak of one without a proper understanding of the other. Do you see what I mean?"

"Of course, but how long will this take and how much will it cost?"

"Ah, Mr. Richard, Hordadef is an honest businessman and will deliver what he has promised as quickly as possible. It shouldn't take more than two weeks, total. However, if you are dissatisfied with any of Hordadef's lessons then I will honor the same agreement for them that we struck regarding last night's lesson, and that is that you will owe me nothing. Certainly nothing can be fairer than that, can it, Mr. Richard? You see, Hordadef is an honest businessman, is he not?"

"Yes, of course. And the guarantee sounds fair enough. But I think under the terms of our so-called contract you must give me some indication of what the total expenses are likely to be, so that I can plan accordingly."

"Well put, Mr. Richard, well put. And so this further agreement is now a part of our contract. As to my services and fees, I can estimate these to be around $300 a day, your most generous tip included, of course. Expenses, though, are a little harder to estimate, but I can tell you that the most significant one will be paying the guards to enter the Pyramid after hours, which will cost $200 an hour, plus generous *baksheesh* for them for allowing us the privilege of private access. So figure $250 to $275 total for this. As to the other expenses, $50 to $100 each day should cover them."

He let out a low whistle as he came to the same conclusion I did: some days would cost me as much as $750. "Mr. Richard, the knowledge you are seeking obviously does not come cheap, but I can assure you, you will be well satisfied with Hordadef's lessons, unlike that university to which you paid so much money in return for apparently so little knowledge. Begging your pardon, of course, for speaking so bluntly."

I sat quietly for a moment. "Thank you for your honesty."

"Honesty? Honesty, Mr. Richard? Why just yesterday, Mr. Richard, you were calling Hordadef a thief, yet today I am an honest man in your eyes! Our contract is a good one and I know that we will both profit from it. Yes, indeed, both will profit and find satisfaction, my friend! Today—"

He slammed on the brakes and simultaneously hit the horn as a car cut in front of us. He leaned his head out the window and shouted a long string of Arabic, although the horn must have drowned it out. Despite his apparent great knowledge, Hordadef was still a cab driver, and a good one at that.

We turned onto the street fronting the Cairo Museum and were swept up in a pure bedlam of vehicles and crowds descending on it from all directions. Progress was excruciatingly slow from that point on, until we managed to find a parking space some twenty minutes later. Hordadef and I got in line for the tickets, which took another twenty minutes, then stood in yet another line waiting to enter.

Hordadef knew the Museum well. He led the way to a display case, in a lightly traveled room on the second floor, which held a number of statues, cups, and mid-sized stones with paintings on them. As I looked at each in turn, Hordadef directed my attention to one in particular, which he said was an image of Ptah. He explained that the earlier Egyptians did not worship such effigies but used them to focus their minds on the underlying aspect of God, which they represented. The earliest Egyptians largely dispensed with such effigies altogether for fear that they might give rise to idolatry. While Egypt recognized many gods and had images for each of them, which depicted their individual divine attributes, all of the attributes in fact belonged to God alone. God can only be contemplated and discussed, however, through the mechanism of his specific attributes, as He is otherwise beyond all human comprehension and understanding. This was the concept behind the multitude and complexity of the pantheon of gods of Egypt, but Hordadef acknowledged that the ancient faith had degenerated into crude idolatry with the passage of time, as men forgot the purpose of the concept. In the end, the original focus of the faith degenerated completely and lapsed into the incessant practice of idolatry and black magic to the exclusion of all else. Faith died and knowledge followed it not long after, for faith and knowledge are one and the same and neither can long survive in the face of such abuse.

As I stared at the painted image, he noted that Ptah was the personification of the Great Seat, which we had discussed last evening by the Pyramid. He was about to continue when a women came into the room, yelling at Hordadef in Arabic. He excused himself for a minute and tried to take the woman aside to talk to her in private, but she would have no part of it and continued to yell at him. He talked to her in a calm tone of voice and, despite her obvious anger, she began to settle down and listen to him. As he spoke he took two $20 bills from his pocket and handed them to her. She accepted them while glaring angrily at him, but then she silently turned and left.

"What was that all about?" I asked.

"The woman is a certified guide, whom I have had encounters with before in here. You see, to guide tourists such as yourself around requires a license from the Museum and I have no such license. She knows that I do not have a license and she was threatening to turn me in and have me banished from coming here in the future, but I persuaded her to accept the money I offered her, instead, and leave us alone, and she consented. And so, Mr. Richard, we now have the matter of this unanticipated but legitimate business expense in dealing with this woman, which we will have to discuss later, man to man." He turned his attention back to the painted image of Ptah.

"Describe for me this painting of Ptah, Mr. Richard."

The image was not unfamiliar. I had seen it in various texts. "This painting depicts the god Ptah, wrapped in full-body-length mumiform clothing with a skull cap, while standing on the symbol for cosmic order. His arms are held tightly at his sides, but are bent at the elbow, level to the ground, and extended in front of him. In his hands he holds a compound staff in front of him with various religious symbols atop it, including the ankh and djed symbols. Behind him, positioned at the base of his neck, is a counterpoise device, called a menat, which was intended to balance the heavy weight of his many pectoral necklaces."

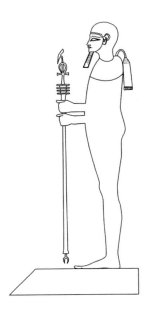

Ptah, Lord of Eternity
Standing on the Symbol for Divine Order
(Adolf Erman, Life in Ancient Egypt; p. 274. After Lepsuis)
Figure 2

"Very good, Mr. Richard. It seems that you did learn something after all from this university you attended. Very good, indeed! Now, Mr. Richard, the reason the god Ptah, the Lord of Eternity, is shown wrapped like this is because he does not move from his position atop the order of the world, which is also true of the Great Seat in the heavens that is located at the center of the visible order of the universe surrounding it. As to the symbols on the staff, which is itself a surveyor's staff used for delineating and marking off the Earth, there are two, both very sacred to ancient Egyptians and both of great significance. The uppermost of the two is the *ankh*, or sacred knot. The second is the *djed* column, which is composed of a column with four parallel lines or circles surrounding it.

"As to the *ankh*, Mr. Richard, it symbolizes the unity of Heaven and Earth; it joins together two apparently separate stems that are bound together into one. This symbol is relevant to the Pyramid, as its location is at the site of the union of Heaven and Earth through the sacred *mer* triangle (54°–36°–90°), which exists between the Pyramid's location and Ptah at its southing culmination altitude: 54°. The *ankh* is the symbol of this unity and it gives its name to the original name of the great city that grew up near the site of the Pyramid, which was called *Ankh-Tawy*, or City of the Sacred Knot, which we remember as Memphis.

"The djed column is the symbol of Osiris, the god of resurrection and rebirth and the Lord of Eternity. When it is lying on its side, it depicts the god in death. When it is raised up after the conclusion of the Osirian Mysteries, it signifies that the god has been raised from the dead and reborn. Of all of the symbols of ancient Egypt, it is by far the most sacred and the most significant. You would do well to remember this and recall it later on, as it will be important to our lesson this evening. It has a profound relationship to the Pyramid and is one of the keys to the knowledge that it holds. Are we agreed?"

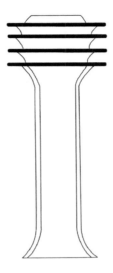

Example of the Sacred *Djed* Column
(R. T. Rundle Clark, Myth and Symbol in Ancient Egypt, Figure 35)
Figure 3

"Yes, of course." My mind was awash with questions that I knew I should probably withhold for the time being, but I had to ask one. "Why did you refer to both Ptah and Osiris as the Lord of Eternity?"

"Both are spoken of as the Lord of Eternity, as is yet a third god, Sokar. The three of them together were the trinity of ancient Memphis, and individually and collectively they were referred to as the Lord of Eternity. It would take too long now to explain why, but in due course you will learn why and that all three are memorialized in the Pyramid."

"Okay."

"Come then, Mr. Richard. You must see one other object, which is located near the entrance to the Museum. I will explain its significance while we are walking, as I will not be able to talk to you about it while we are looking at it because of the guide issue. Do you understand?"

"Yes."

"Well then, let us proceed to it. The statue that we will see is undoubtedly a very familiar one to you. It is a seated statue of the Pharaoh Zoser, one of the earliest kings of Egypt and the builder of the famous step pyramid at Saqqara. Do you know this statue?"

"Of course."

"Very good, then. When we see it, I want you to remember its eyes and the headdress it wears, because we will talk of these things at a future date."

As we neared the entrance, Hordadef slowed his pace in front of the statue. It had gaping holes where its eyes once were, and it wore the nemeses head cloth that all subsequent pharaohs of Egypt wore until the end of the pharaonic age. The statue was a famous one and had formerly sat in the step pyramid complex at Saqqara until it was removed here to the Museum for safekeeping and replaced with a copy. The eyes had obviously been of some expensive material and were gouged out long ago for their perceived value in some ancient marketplace. I turned to look at Hordadef and he motioned to me that we should exit. Outside the Museum I asked why he found these particular features of the statue so intriguing and he told me to remember the question for a future lesson.

On our way back to the hotel we stopped at an inexpensive diner for a late lunch. I picked up the tab. After all, it was a legitimate business expense. We arrived at the hotel around four o'clock. Hordadef stopped the car, and when he came around to open the door for me he said that we had a reservation at ten that night to visit the interior of the Pyramid. As he reentered the car, he said he would call for me around half past nine and that I should be prompt. I said I would be and he drove off. I spent the next several hours enjoying the pool and wondering what the evening would hold for us. I was looking forward to it, to say the least.

* * *

I ate supper at eight o'clock and then went back to my room to get my camera and put on mosquito repellant. I waited for Hordadef just inside the hotel gates at quarter past nine. I heard him call my name as he came inside the gates to greet me. He met the stares of the hotel guard with silence and the two of us turned and left the grounds. I discreetly handed him $300 in twenty-dollar bills for the guards as we walked to the cab. We drove up the hill and stopped in front of the guardhouse. Hordadef went inside and reemerged seconds later. He turned and waved to the guards as we drove off. At the top of the hill Hordadef turned the car toward the Pyramid and parked not far from it.

For a moment we stood before the vast structure, silhouetted against the night sky.

"I never tire of coming here, Mr. Richard. Never."

Out of the shadows to our left came two guards from the Antiquities Service. Hordadef noticed them, too, and approached them. There was some quick conversation and laughter, then the guards energetically shook hands with Hordadef. He waved at them as he returned to my side. "Everything is nicely arranged, Mr. Richard. We should have a good visit and I hope you're ready for it."

"Indeed I am."

"Well, then, as soon as the other party comes out, the Pyramid is all ours for one hour. Do you have any questions?"

"No, none at the moment, but I'm sure I will have many later on. Are we going to see the terrestrial globe and celestial spheres?"

He laughed faintly. "We'll see. Now, Mr. Richard, you must know that to the Egyptians the number four was the numerical symbol for the Earth. Do not ask me why now because you'll find out for yourself shortly. Just remember it."

The earlier party, composed of several dozen Westerners, came out of the Pyramid talking loudly. The surrounding darkness soon swallowed them up but their voices could still be heard, trailing them as they left. The guards motioned for us to enter. As we ducked to clear the low passageway, I could feel the accumulated heat from the multitudes of people who had visited the structure earlier in the day. I found this a little surprising, as I had expected the interior of the Pyramid to be cooler than the outside temperature, but the opposite was true.

We clambered up the Ascending Passage, frequently bumping our heads on its low ceiling. Suddenly the passage ended and the soaring height of the Grand Gallery opened dramatically over us. This feature of the Pyramid never ceased to amaze me, and I stared up at its high ceiling with opened-mouthed awe. In front of me, Hordadef silently climbed the wooden stairway that had been installed in the Grand Gallery to permit access to the upper chambers of the Pyramid. I couldn't help but notice that he did not seem to have the same interest in the Grand Gallery as I did. Whatever the reason, when he reached the top he turned and waited for me. I quickly joined him and was about to say something when he ducked again and entered the antechamber to the King's Chamber. I bent and followed him until he stopped, and we both stood there in the faint light. He pointed to the four inscribed vertical lines that marked the stone over the entryway.

"Look, Mr. Richard, do you see? Four lines. Interesting, no?"

Before I could answer he had stooped and entered the short passageway to the King's Chamber. I followed right behind. Seconds later we were both standing fully erect in the spaciousness of the King's Chamber, which echoed faintly to our footsteps. The light inside the chamber was harsh but permitted easy viewing of the details.

The King's Chamber, the inner sanctum of the Pyramid, has been subject to extensive measurement and investigation, and endless speculation as to its purpose over the ages. Napoleon visited it during his campaign in Egypt, spending a terrifying period of time alone it, which he steadfastly declined to ever discuss. John Greaves, an English astronomer, measured it in the seventeenth century, looking for measurements of the Earth that it was long rumored to contain. The data that he collected was of very great interest amongst the scientists of the time; even Sir Isaac Newton consulted it in his work.

And, of course, treasure hunters and explorers throughout the ages have entered it: Al-Mamun, a ninth-century Caliph of Bagdad (who was supposedly the first to visit it since it was built thousands of years before); Howard Vyse (who used dynamite to explore it); Piazzi Smyth, Astronomer Royal of Scotland (who measured every inch of it in pursuit of support for his controversial theories); Williams Flinders Petrie, the father of modern Egyptology (who explored and measured it extensively in order to refute Smyth's theories); and so on and on.

Now Hordadef and I had it all to ourselves.

What further secrets does it hold? I wondered. "Pretty scary, isn't it, being all alone in a grave at night?" I asked.

"Mr. Richard, no man was ever buried here." Hordadef strolled along the south wall, pointing up as he moved, turning and gesturing all about. "Do you see, Mr. Richard, four lines dividing the five courses of stone along each wall?" My eyes followed the movements of his arm, but I didn't know what to say in response. "Sit, Mr. Richard, sit here," he said as motioned for me to sit down near the center of the chamber while he lowered himself to the spot. I sat, still looking all about.

"Hordadef, I don't see any globes or spheres here, so they must be a figment of one of your stories."

"Mr. Richard, all is here as Hordadef promised. You must be patient, though." He removed a small notebook from his pocket and sketched an outline of the Pyramid. Then he drew a half circle around it, using the apex as a radius. "There, Mr. Richard, do you not see the terrestrial globe?"

I stared at him for a moment, then sarcastically retorted, "Excuse me, excuse me, Mr. Hordadef, but I did not enter into a contract with you to learn such nonsense. You have shown me nothing that many people have not long known through many different sources."

Hordadef had a slightly puzzled look on his face and sat for a moment without moving or saying a word. Then he burst out laughing, threw his head back, and rolled over onto his side. He continued laughing for a full minute, and I laughed with him at the obvious joke. Then he sat upright again and wiped the tears from his eyes.

"That was very good, Mr. Richard, very good indeed!" He shook his head. "Mr. Richard, above our heads are situated a series of four chambers that mark off four horizontal lines. Above them is a fifth chamber, but this has no significance and was designed only to preserve the structures under it from the crushing weight above. From where we sit to the uppermost of the four lines is the pillar of Osiris, and the four lines formed in stone above are the four lines of the *djed* pillar. This is the *djed* pillar raised up for all time. It is Osiris, raised up from the dead and restored to life.

"Before we proceed further, you must understand that there is an order and harmony between Heaven and Earth that is also reflected in the soul of man. This was by God's design at the act of creation. The Pyramid records the knowledge of this Divine Order in its stones and is a testament to God that man understands these things. It also preserves this knowledge that man might remember and not forget. Every aspect of the Pyramid speaks to this, and it is the true purpose of the Pyramid. Remember this, Mr. Richard, remember it; otherwise, you will only see the Pyramid as so many others do—just an impressive heap of stone reared up to serve man's vanity—which is a profound error. A most profound error, indeed. This is why you must read and reread the writing on the small piece of paper that I gave you the other night. Everything else that I will relate to you stems from this understanding.

"Now Mr. Richard, observe closely," he said as he raised his small pad of paper back up with its outline of the Pyramid surrounded by a semicircle. He drew in the King's Chamber and the four horizontal lines of the four chambers above it. Next he drew a horizontal line from the uppermost of the four lines until it cut the semicircle to either side of it. He then drew a vertical line up through the middle of the four lines until it crossed over the outline of the Pyramid, and then a second vertical line from this until it cut the semicircle to either side of it, as had the line below it.

"Now, Mr. Richard, we can draw the other half of the Earth if you'd like and produce two other similar lines from the inverted mirror image of the Pyramid, but it is not necessary. However, you should know that four lines, four parallel lines are produced in this fashion. Now can you tell me what these two lines represent?"

I stared at his drawing for a moment and said, "It looks like the polar circle and the Tropic of Cancer."

"Very good, Mr. Richard! Observe, please." He drew my attention once more to the drawing on the pad. "The lower line is indeed the Tropic of Cancer and it defines the upper limit of the Sun's apparent movements as it travels about the Earth, reaching it on the longest day of the year in the northern hemisphere—the summer solstice—before turning and heading south again. The upper line marks the apparent path followed by Ptah as it forever circles about the North celestial pole and the north pole of the axis of the Earth below it. These two lines and the two similar lines of the southern hemisphere mark the four great lines or rings of the Earth. And in case you are wondering, the stones above us were set to very great precision to generate these lines as accurately as possible (see source of measurements in Appendix 2). Now do you observe the Terrestrial Globe, Mr. Richard? You see, it is still here, just as it has been since the Pyramid was built."

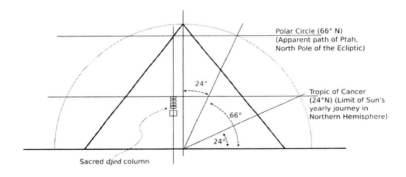

The Terrestrial Globe

Figure 4

I had to admit it was stunning. I thought that the globe, if it existed, would contain maps of the Earth, but how simplistic and unimaginative that would have been. Far better to capture the essential motions of the Earth in relation to the heavens, instead, which is what the globe in the Pyramid did. Knowing orientation, direction, and measures of time and distance, one can travel to any place on Earth and return. Maps are merely recordkeeping devices.

As I stared at the drawing, the significance of the structures above the King's Chamber seemed so obvious now that Hordadef had explained them. How clever were the architects and builders to have incorporated such a complex model into the Pyramid's structure. Here was the key to one of the greatest mysteries concerning the Pyramid. The legends were true then: there was a terrestrial globe in the Pyramid, just as they had spoken of! I was tempted to ask Hordadef about the celestial spheres, but I decided not to, as I was certain he would show them to me in due time. Still, my mind was in full flight, wondering what else might still lie hidden in the venerable ancient structure.

"Now, Mr. Richard, you see that the *djed* column, the great symbol of Osiris, the god of resurrection and rebirth, the Lord of Eternity, is here, standing forever upright. And as you have observed, it is a model Earth itself that derives from the location and arrangement of the *djed* symbol in the Pyramid. It, too, can be said to be standing upright forever. Do you agree?"

"Of course. I understand."

"Good! Now can we not also say that the Pyramid is Osiris, who is the Earth? Do you not see that here, all are one and the same?"

"Yes."

"Very well, then. Do you remember the statue that we observed earlier in the Museum, of the god Ptah?"

"Yes, of course."

"Then you no doubt recall the counterpoise that the statue had mounted at the back of its neck, which you said was meant to balance the weight of the many necklaces it wore. This is not the purpose of the device, Mr. Richard. You see, Ptah holds the *djed* upright, to symbolize that he is holding the Earth upright, and the counterweight helps him to balance the weight of the Earth, not the necklaces. It is important that you remember these things, for as I said last night, Ptah as the Great Seat is the center of the universe, and all order stems from Him. As long as Ptah holds the Earth upright, there will be order between Heaven and Earth, and life will continue until the end of time. When Heaven removes this order, life will be extinguished and time will end. Do you agree?"

"Yes."

"Very good, then. I think our time here is nearly up." He leaned back, raising his head slightly, and looked all about the chamber with a smile. "It is truly a wonder, is it not, Mr. Richard?"

I said nothing as I, too, was looking about the chamber and admiring its simple lines and the sense of timelessness imparted by the great stones of granite all about us. Here we were, in the very heart of what was quite possibly the most sublime monument ever raised by the hand of man. What secrets had it once held? What secrets did it still hold? My imagination ran wild, and I might have continued to entertain such thoughts had not Hordadef interrupted them by rising and stating that we should start back. I looked up at him and wanted to ask if we could stay for a few more minutes. Instead I rose to leave. But as I did so, he paused to say he'd almost forgotten something.

"Please, Mr. Richard, count the numbers of courses of stones that make up the floor of the chamber." I was a little puzzled but looked behind me and counted two, and then walked to the opposite wall counting four more. I turned to him.

"There are six, but why do you ask?"

"Remember that number because we will discuss it later, along with the purpose of the arrangement of the floor. It is related to Osiris and to one of the two other triangles that I mentioned last night."

At the top step of the Grand Gallery, Hordadef paused and asked if I knew what this chamber had been used for. The conventional explanation held that it was used in the funerary procession to add drama to the burial of the Pharaoh, but I suspected from Hordadef's line of thought that this was unlikely. So I offered him the alternate theory of its purpose, which held that it was once used as an observatory.

"Very good, Mr. Richard. That university education of yours did provide you with some useful knowledge, after all. At one time there was a great machine here that was used to mark the declination of the stars as they passed the midpoint of the long, narrow aperture above us. This machine has long since disappeared, but you can envision it moving up and down the incline of the space and locking into the slots located along the walls, as necessary. A clock recorded the exact moment of transit across the centerline of the aperture, which measured the right ascension for each of the stars. Then, by using the measured declination and right ascension for each star and planet, observers created accurate star charts. This is probably way beyond you and it is really not necessary that you grasp these concepts for the purposes of our lesson. Just understand that this chamber was used for astronomical observations and that a great machine formerly stood in this space for this purpose. I cannot say for certain what happened to it, but we can assume its design and purpose from the arrangement of the stones in this chamber, can we not?"

"It seems so, Hordadef," I said as I looked up at the ceiling of the gallery, high above us.

He stepped forward and was heading down the stairs when I called after him, "Were these star charts the celestial spheres that we spoke of yesterday?"

"No. Those are an entirely different matter and are located elsewhere in the Pyramid, Mr. Richard. We'll save those for another night, as there are a few more things that I must teach you before we speak of them."

So it's true, then. The spheres did exist! I thought to myself. I couldn't wait to see them!

He continued downstairs and out of the Pyramid in silence. I followed, still amazed at what I had learned. Once outside, we continued to the car and drove back down to the hotel, where I opened the door and climbed out before he could park. "So, Mr. Richard, we have learned much today and you will see that we will learn just as much tomorrow. Let us meet early in the morning, as we will be driving down to see one of the other pyramids located south of here and it would be best for us to leave early to avoid traffic. Shall we say seven o'clock?"

"Seven it is. I'll see you then. Have a nice night."

"Ah, Mr. Richard, aren't we forgetting something?"

I looked back at him with momentary puzzlement before remembering that I hadn't paid him yet. "How could I forget?" I handed him the bills. "I hope this meets with your satisfaction."

"Most assuredly so, Mr. Richard. And good evening to you, too, my friend. Things are going very well with our contract, do you not agree?"

"Indeed they are, Hordadef. Indeed they are."

"Oh, and bring a jacket, Mr. Richard, as it will probably be a little cold in the morning."

He waved from the cab and tapped his horn lightly as he drove off into the night.

4

Divine Order: Measures of Time and Distance

The next day I rose early, ate a quick breakfast, and actually waited for Hordadef to arrive instead of finding him already there. I didn't have to wait long.

"Good morning, Mr. Richard. I trust you slept well and are ready for more of Hordadef's stories of Egypt."

"Good morning to you, too. I am fully rested and eager to proceed. If today's stories are anything like yesterday's, it should be a fascinating adventure. So where are we off to?"

"The step pyramid of *Zawiyet el-Aryan*. Have you heard of it?"

"Yes, I have, but it is usually not on most visitors' itineraries. There's not much to it or truly significant about it. Why did you pick it for a visit, if I might ask?"

"Ah, you are no longer just a sightseer, Mr. Richard, but a student of Hordadef, and the pyramid there will help with today's lesson. That's why we're going."

His answer was reassuring. Yet I couldn't help wondering why he had picked such an obscure pyramid when others nearby were far more famous and seemingly far more interesting, as well. But I was completely in Hordadef's control after the last night's experience in the Pyramid. The whole thing still utterly amazed me. As the coolness of the morning air rushed over me through the cab's open windows, I relived the whole experience in my mind. I didn't get too deep into my thoughts before Hordadef started talking again.

"I brought some food and water for us today. There are no stores in the area, so I took the liberty of purchasing some in Cairo. Legitimate business expense, Mr. Richard. Also, I brought some flashlights and rope in case we need them. No charge for them, though," he added, laughing.

We'd gone south on the main road only about five miles when Hordadef turned right and headed for the desert hills not far off the main road. We were soon under a dense stand of palm trees, and among a number of small houses and shops. Hordadef pulled into a driveway. He stopped the car and got out but told me to wait—that he'd only be a minute or two. He disappeared around the side of the house.

A short while later he came back toward the car with a middle-aged man, the two of them talking and laughing as they walked. They stopped short of the car and turned to face one another. There was more conversation, more laughter, the kissing of cheeks and farewells, and then they turned and walked away from one another.

Hordadef got back in the car and started it up. As he backed out of the driveway he said, "That was the guardian of the pyramid. Had to pay him for our visit and give him some *baksheesh*. Another business expense, Mr. Richard, but he gave me the key so we can stay as long as we want. Not like the Great Pyramid, where the clock runs and you have to pay close attention to it. We've got this pyramid all to ourselves today."

"Hordadef, I have a question."

"Please ask it, Mr. Richard."

"Are you the guardian of the Great Pyramid?"

"Am I the *what*? Do you see Hordadef wearing a uniform or walking around waiting for *baksheesh*? Of course not. I am a simple cab driver and no more."

"And so you are, but you know an awful lot about it. And while you may not be its physical guardian, it seems you could be its intellectual guardian. Are you?"

"What is an intellectual guardian, Mr. Richard? I have never heard this term."

"Someone who is entrusted with knowledge about a particular thing and keeps its memory alive."

"I have never heard of such a thing. Not in Egypt, anyhow. Perhaps there is such a position in the Antiquities Authority, but I am not aware of it."

I wanted to pursue the issue, but Hordadef swung the car up against some broken bricks that stood between a parking area and the desert beyond and was quickly out of the car. I dropped the issue for the time being.

We walked into the desert a short distance, arriving at the ruins of a nondescript step pyramid that ostensibly had never been completed. We walked around its southern base a few moments, staring at the structure. When Hordadef said he wanted to climb it, we stopped and scrambled to the top, which was covered with sand that made it almost indistinguishable from the surrounding desert. He paused at the top of the low-slung structure, surveying the surrounding area to the north. Then he turned to me and said that we were standing on one of the oldest structures in Egypt and that it had once been used for astronomical observations.

"This, Mr. Richard, was an *ahket,* or horizon. The priests of old, who were called *watchers,* used this structure—and others like it that have long since disappeared—to observe and measure the movements of the stars. They stood along the first step of the edge of the structure and used its upper surface as an artificial horizon to measure the altitude and azimuth of individual stars."

He stopped and looked at me for a second and then began again, sensing that I may not have understood him. He extended his right arm and pointed it toward the northern horizon.

"True north is the beginning reference point for making observations of the stars. To make measurements of them, all proceed in the same way. First, you measure a star's height above the horizon, or its altitude, and denote the reading as having been taken from either the northern or southern half of the celestial dome," which he demonstrated by raising his arm slowly along a vertical arc from the northern horizon to about a 45° angle above his head. "That is 45° north. Then you measure its azimuth, or horizontal arc from north," which he demonstrated by moving his arm to the left along the horizon, to a spot about 45° to the left from north.

"It's really quite simple. Altitude is angular measure above the horizon," which he demonstrated again by repeatedly raising and lowering his arm from the horizon to various angles above it. Then he demonstrated azimuth again, by repeatedly swinging his arm and pointing to various angles to the left and right of true north along the horizon. He called out several combinations of altitude and azimuth angles and pointed at them to reinforce his point.

"Measuring a star's or a planet's altitude and azimuth, and marking the time of the observation, was the habitual practice of the watcher priests since time immemorial in recording the movements of the heavenly bodies. It was a practice followed by priests everywhere for this purpose.

"Now, Mr. Richard, man perceives the sky as a great dome above his head or sphere about the Earth, with all points on it seemingly at the same distance from him, do you agree?"

"Yes."

"Well, then, this dome or sphere is composed of an infinite number of points, each defined by its individual altitude and azimuth reading. In other words, it is defined by number, is it not?"

"I guess if you mean that each point can be plotted by its altitude and azimuth readings, as measured in degrees, then that sounds correct."

"Precisely! That is the key for establishing a reference grid for all domes and spheres, including the celestial sphere. And the process works in reverse, too. If someone knows the altitude and azimuth measures of a particular point, its location can readily be found on the dome."

He smiled at me and said I was showing real promise. I was almost too embarrassed to tell him that at times I struggled to keep up with him, even though he appeared to be making extraordinary efforts to help me understand. He put his arm around my shoulders and pointed his left arm to the northern sky.

"If Polaris, or the North Star, was visible now and we could measure its altitude here and then compare the reading to the one at the Pyramid's location, it would be a little lower in the sky." He turned and said that if we were to continue to travel south, it would drop lower still on the horizon until we reached the equator, where it would appear to rest right on the horizon. And then he turned and faced north again and said if we walked toward the North Pole, the North celestial pole would appear to rise up in the heavens until it stood directly overhead at the pole. He admitted that he was repeating himself but said he needed to do so. The changing angular location of the North celestial pole was of critical interest to the watcher priests because it related directly to the measures of degrees of latitude and distance.

"Now this distance between degrees of earthly latitude was both measurable and constant, which gave them the beginning reference point for a universal system of measure. The distance in one degree of latitude was divided into sixty units called geographic miles, which were further divided into finer and finer terms of measure, called cubits and feet. However, all of this originally came from watching the heavens and specifically the changes in the altitude of the North celestial pole, as one moved north or south."

It was tough to accept all of that, but I did for the time being and said nothing. Besides, I hardly knew where to begin with any questions I might have had.

"I think we're done here, Mr. Richard." Hordadef began walking back down the mound to the edge of the structure. I followed along behind and we climbed down together. While he brushed his hands together to remove the dust, he set out for the edge of the structure, saying we had one more part of the ruin to visit.

We walked along the eastern edge of the structure to its northern end, where we found an iron gate lying across an ancient stairway that led down into the passages under the pyramid.

Hordadef stopped short. "Ah me! I forgot our coats and flashlights. You wait here and I'll be right back." He quickly followed the faint path to the parking lot and returned in moments with our gear. He bent down to unlock the gate with the key that he had received earlier from the guardian in the village.

"Be careful, Mr. Richard. This place has few visitors, so we might run into some snakes or bats or other wild animals. Also, some of the stone is worn and damaged in spots, so watch your step."

We headed down a steep flight of steps (which hardly merited the term, they were so uneven, giving the whole descent the feel of a controlled slide). We switched on the flashlights midway and Hordadef warned me that the stairs ended in a steep drop-off. At that point we should find a ladder. He shone the light down the stairway and we distinctly saw the ends of the ladder in the light just ahead of us. He reached the ladder first and, as he stepped onto it, as if on cue several bats flew past. Hordadef laughed and said he would understand if I wanted to turn back. I thought about it but said no. If there were several there had to be more, and sure enough bats soon flew around our heads with some regularity during our descent.

At the bottom Hordadef said we needed to take the ladder with us, so we placed our flashlights on the floor and pulled it down. Then we retrieved the flashlights and proceeded along a littered passageway toward an area of sunlight illuminating the darkened passageway just ahead of us. The light came down a fairly broad, square shaft, which descended from the desert surface above. As I looked up the shaft, Hordadef motioned for me to help him raise the ladder. I noticed that a dark passageway continued toward the pyramid and pointed my flashlight down it, about to ask Hordadef if that was the way to the burial chamber. But he told me to hold the ladder while he climbed up to another passageway above us that also led in the direction of the pyramid.

As I held the ladder I noticed a few more bats flying about the passageways and quickly turned from them to watch Hordadef climb. He swung off the ladder into the passageway above and gave a slight cry as several dozen bats flew out of it. He swung back onto the ladder and climbed back down to me.

"Let's go back outside," he said as he reached the foot. "I don't think either of us will be comfortable with all of this activity."

We returned to the entrance stairway, where we raised the ladder into its original position. We climbed up the ladder and the adjoining stairway to the desert above.

"Well, those were some Egyptians I had hoped to avoid," Hordadef laughed as he replaced the gate with a loud bang and restored the lock.

"Come, Mr. Richard." We approached the opening in the shaft, where we had stood moments ago, just close enough to see about halfway down but not the bottom. "Come. Let's sit here under the shade of the pyramid for a moment."

As we sat down, he asked if I minded him smoking and I said no. He lit a cigarette and enjoyed a few puffs. Then he gestured with the lit cigarette toward the shaft and asked if I knew what it was for. I told him that it was probably used to lower the king's sarcophagus and burial furniture to the passageways below. He took another drag, shaking his head lightly up and down. "You've been reading too much archaeology. That is the Well-of-the-Sun, or rather it was *a* Well-of-the-Sun. There were a number of them in ancient times in Egypt, when they were used to record the movements of the Sun, particularly the time of its maximum daily rise in the heavens."

He pointed out that the watcher priests could recognize this exact moment when facing north, since the northern, eastern, and western sides of the shaft were all illuminated at that one instant. The watchers observed the movements of the Sun from the upper passageway off the vertical shaft— the one we had attempted to reach before the bats drove us out. The Sun penetrated deeper and deeper into the well as the longest day of the year approached until on the summer solstice it reached maximum penetration down the well before retreating back up the shaft. The phenomenon in modern terms, he said, was called *local apparent noon*.

"This was one of the most important observations of the watcher priests, who lived and worked at this structure for many years until it became obsolete."

Each day they rose from the rooms located along the passageways below to observe stars in the morning, then record the time and bearing of sunrise. Next they observed local apparent noon. In the evening they observed sunset, and then the stars again as they appeared during evening twilight. Five observations each day, day in and day out, without fail. This was the beginning of the measurement of time, for the timing of events that repeated themselves with such regularity was of obvious importance to them. They noticed the return of the solstices and equinoxes year after year, and the return of the stars to their same position in the heavens with the same regularity. This gave rise to the calendar, and later to clocks for counting fine time in hours, minutes, and seconds.

"Time is a most curious thing. But in essence, time is motion and motion is time, and since motion relates to distance, that too is time," Hordadef said.

He looked at me as I looked down at my watch, and he placed his hand over it. "This, Mr. Richard, is artificial time, based on the movements of the Sun. It is not movement, but recordkeeping. Do you understand?"

"No, not really."

"Well, if the Sun were to cease moving, would time continue?"

"Of course not."

"Well, then, motion is necessary to the existence of time, is it not?"

"Yes," I said, but I felt as if he were overwhelming me again, and this time with facts that appeared to have little or no relationship to the Pyramid. I wanted to tell him that I didn't see the connection but I kept quiet.

"And this is the reason that Ptah, or the Great Seat, is said to exist beyond time, since it never has nor will have motion, as long as God permits the universe to continue. All of the other areas of heaven and the celestial bodies that lie in them are in continuous motion, from which time is computed and measured, except for the Great Seat, which lies at the center of all. It can't be measured and time has no meaning when it comes to describing it; it simply is and always will be.

"Time is a circle, as the motions that define it continue to return to their former positions in the heavens. And it is the circle, with its 360°, that is the starting point for defining the measures of time. All measures of time are derived from this number or were defined so as to fit within it as a perfect multiple. The reasons for this are somewhat involved and I would be only too happy to explain them to you, if you'd like."

I had a feeling he was testing me and my attention, but the subject was growing somewhat tiresome. "No, it is not necessary."

He smiled in response, but his look was tinged with doubt, which made me feel very self-conscious of my growing impatience. "We'll skip over most of the details then, but there are several that you must understand. The first has to do with the measure of the relationship of fine clock time to the measure of time by the ages. And the second has to do with the measure of time in terms of man's clock, or how his life is defined in terms of time.

"All motions in time are also factors of the number 432. This was by design. The Egyptians had a fascination with harmonizing all measures according to the perceived Divine Order of the universe, which they believed was reflected throughout all of creation, including the motions of heaven and Earth—and of man himself. The key to this order, they believed, was the number 432.

"For example, there are 43,200 seconds in half a day. And this same figure relates to the clock of a man, which is based on the number 72: 72 years of life, 72 pulse beats per minute. Now, 72 years is also equal to the amount of time it takes for the North celestial pole to move 1°, which when multiplied by 60 (60 X 72) equals 4,320 years. There's that number 432 again, Mr. Richard," he said as he smiled at me.

"Man's pulse rate of 72 beats per minute is related to time and motion and distance—all of these. You remember earlier when I told you the source for measure was the distance between two consecutive degrees of latitude? Well, 72 pulse beats per minute is directly related to that figure, too. You see, in ancient times the distance that a man could comfortably walk in a day was figured at 30 miles, or half a degree of latitude, which was called a march because it was the motion of a man as measured in distance and time. A march was equivalent to 12 hours of walking with 2 hours for rest, for a total of 10 hours of motion. Now, these 10 hours of motion, when multiplied by 60 minutes per hour times 72 pulse beats per minute, is equal to 43,200, which is the same number of seconds in half a day of Sun time. This was a fundamental measure of distance and enabled men to equate the distance traveled to the time necessary to complete it, which permitted him to not only explore areas far removed from him and to return, but also permitted him to record their locations. Therefore, time is not only motion, but distance as well, Mr. Richard. However, keep in mind that this 72 pulse beats per minute equates to clock time and not the actual pulse beat experienced by a man when walking, which of course would be higher."

He smiled at me as he pointed out that in the pulse-beat measure of distance there again was the number 432 but I was growing tired of the whole subject. The expression on his face showed that he was quite pleased with himself and his presentation, and he must have believed that I should have felt grateful for the lesson. I didn't. That it all was of little or no interest to me was an understatement.

"Well, Mr. Richard, why don't we get something to eat for lunch and head back to the Pyramid? I have one last thing to tell you today."

"That sounds good to me."

We stopped briefly to drop the key off with the guardian and then headed back toward Giza. I sat silently, lost in the faint haze of the Egyptian landscape, which is caused by the atmosphere's suffusion with moisture from the Nile's evaporation, giving it an almost dreamlike quality. If I had any impression of this morning's activities, it was that my time had been wasted.

During our lunch in a small restaurant just outside Cairo, Hordadef spoke in animated tones about the morning's adventures, particularly the experience with the bats, under the pyramid. I laughed along with him. But when he brought up our conversations about the measures of time and distance, I sat quietly. It really didn't interest me.

We arrived back at the hotel around three o'clock in the afternoon. Hordadef was obviously excited to be heading back to the Pyramid, but I found it hard to join in his enthusiasm. I reluctantly accompanied him and he talked the whole way up the plateau about how much he had enjoyed our morning together. When we reached the top we stood away from the crowds of people and looked at it without talking for a minute.

Then he turned to me and asked what I thought of the things that he had told me that morning. I replied almost without thinking. "Well, if that was any indication of the quality of the stories that you have left to tell me, then perhaps I should invoke the provision in our contract that gives me the option of not paying if I'm dissatisfied with the lesson."

"Excuse me. Excuse me, Mr. Richard. Dissatisfied? Do you even appreciate what I have told you?"

"No, not really. How is all of that time and distance stuff connected to the Pyramid, and what I'm looking for and paying you to teach me?"

"Not satisfied?" he repeated. "Not satisfied?"

He appeared genuinely hurt by my words. I was thinking how to apologize when he directed me to draw on the desert at our feet the six courses of stone from the King's Chamber.

"Excuse me? What are you talking about?" Then it dawned on me! I recalled his telling me to count the courses of stone on the floor of the King's Chamber just before we left it the night before, and that they had indeed totaled six. I was about to ask him to repeat his instruction, but before I could his foot scratched in the sand before me six roughly spaced lines, all facing the Pyramid.

"Now, Mr. Richard, these six spaces represent Osiris in his name of the Great Circle, the Great Surround, the Ring that encircles the Outer Most Lands—words from the walls of the later pyramids, the pyramid texts, Mr. Richard. These six spaces, or segments, combined are the Great Circle, or the equator of the Earth. Look at the Pyramid, Mr. Richard. The second 45°–90°–45° triangle that we spoke of the other night lies in this direction."

He extended his forearms at equal angles from his sides toward the Pyramid. "From its location here at 30° north it is 1,800 miles from the equator, and the diagonals of its base cut along 45° arms to the equator—the Great Circle of the Earth, the Ring that Surrounds the Outer Most Lands—where they mark off a 3,600-mile segment." He moved his arms up and down with a pronounced chopping motion. "Now, 3,600 multiplied by 6 gives the circumference of the Earth in miles: 21,600 geographic miles. The Egyptians were able to calculate this from their knowledge of the characteristics of 45° right triangles. So, once again, Mr. Richard, there is your terrestrial sphere, or another facet of it—in this case the measure of the equator—and there again is the unity and harmony of the Pyramid with Heaven and Earth.

"When the Sun reaches the equinox, it moves directly along the path of the equator and its rise and run can be observed and measured directly. And when it reaches local apparent noon at this location on that day, it stands at an altitude of 60° south, viewed from the Pyramid. This is the second occurrence of the 30°–60°–90° triangle that I spoke of the other night, and which I told you we would speak of later.

"One thing is even more important, though. In this position at 60° altitude the Sun makes a perfect equilateral triangle with this location at 30° north and its counterpart in the southern hemisphere at 30° south, from where the Sun also stands at an altitude of 60° at that same precise moment (Figure #5). This is not a coincidence and demonstrates once more that the location of the Pyramid was chosen by design, and its purpose was to mark the harmony of this location with Heaven. For this triangle is the very symbol of Heaven. From the equilateral triangle arises one of the numbering systems for time, which is based on the number 60.

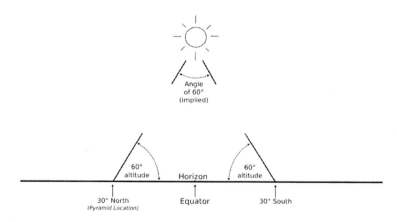

The Perfect Triangle (60°-60°-60°)
(Created by the Sun's location on the equator at the equinox,
at Local Apparent Noon, with 30°N and 30°S)

Figure 5

"I should mention several more facts, Mr. Richard, particularly since you seem to have found all of the numbers I mentioned to you this morning not worthy of your interest. The distance of 3,600 miles, marked off by the diagonals of the Pyramid's base, exactly encompasses two great ages, or 4,320 years, of the great calendar of 25,920 years, which is based on the precession of the equinoxes along the ecliptic, the apparent path of the Sun around the Earth. Also, during this same 4,320-year period, the North celestial pole moves along its circular path about the Great Seat exactly 1/6 of its circuit, which also takes 25,920 years to complete.

"So, then, the Great Circle of Osiris that is the equator of the Earth is reflected in the Great Circle of Heaven above, the white walls of Heaven. Is it not, Mr. Richard? And these two great circles, the one around the Earth and the other around the Great Seat of Ptah in the heavens, are the very embodiment of infinity, as these two great cosmic serpents of time each move head-to-tail in the endless motion imparted to them by God Himself at the beginning of time. Once again we see demonstrated here the unity that exists between the Pyramid and Heaven and Earth. Are we not agreed, Mr. Richard?

"And one more number involving 432 and the Pyramid! The Pyramid has a surface area on each of its four visible faces that stands in relation to the surface area of the Earth itself, at a scale of 1/43,200.

"Another fact, Mr. Richard! When the Sun runs along the equator at the equinox, the diagonals of the Pyramid not only mark off a geographic distance of 3,600 miles, they also mark off one watch of time, or 4 hours, which again if multiplied by the 6 segments of the floor yields a day of 24 hours.

"And finally, based on their knowledge of the dimensions of the Earth and measures of time, the Egyptians were able to determine that the apparent velocity of the Sun as it travels along the equator, and the actual rotational velocity of the Earth at the equator, is a constant 1,000 Egyptian geographic cubits per second.

"So you see, the Pyramid marks not only the measurements of the Earth but also time, and relates them to one another. It sits silently witnessing and measuring the passing not only of the hours of the day but of the great ages as well

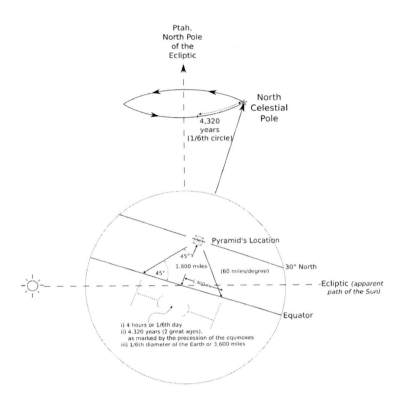

Measures of Time and Distance
(Generated by Pyramid's Diagonals)

Figure 6

My mind was in total turmoil. I grasped the importance of what he was saying, but I couldn't fully comprehend its meaning. Instead of finding reason to be bored that morning, I now regretted that I had not paid closer attention to him and tried to appreciate more fully what he was telling me. The full magnitude of it may have had an even greater impact.

I stared up at the Pyramid, nodding my head in response to his question but feeling almost embarrassed by my inattention earlier. Here again, indeed, was direct evidence of the terrestrial sphere contained in or rather defined by the Pyramid. As I looked at the vast structure, the terrestrial globe it generated in my mind appeared to readily transform into the Earth itself, and then without pause into the motions of the heavens above. It was a bewildering spectacle to behold, almost surreal in its effect on me. I could hear Hordadef speaking of the number 432 as my mind's eye continued to contemplate the display before it. In that instant I felt as though the centuries that stood between me and the Pyramid melted away and I suddenly had an understanding of it and a connection to it that I had never known before. It was at once personal and primordial in its power. The measures of time, distance, and life itself all seemed vitally connected. All I could do was stare and foolishly wag my head up and down as Hordadef continued to talk, but I could no longer focus on his words.

I stood in silence for several minutes before noticing that Hordadef, too, was staring up at the Pyramid. "Do you now see that the Pyramid, the Earth, and Heaven are all one? And do you now see that the Pyramid stands here in perfect harmony with Heaven and Earth, as it silently bears witness to the passing of the ages?"

"Yes."

"Then surely you have found satisfaction in today's lesson and are no longer interested in cheating a simple cab driver out of what is due to him by contract?"

Unexpectedly my flight of fancy was at an end. I looked at him, almost without comprehension.

"Very well then, Mr. Richard. I think we are finished for the day. Why don't we head back down so you can enjoy yourself, maybe take a swim in the hotel pool, have a couple of drinks, and get ready for tomorrow?"

"Of course, that sounds good to me." I walked beside him back down the plateau. He continued to make small talk, but my thoughts were still on the Pyramid and the visions it summoned. What a wonder!

When we reached the hotel he stopped and said, "I'll pick you up at eight in the morning, then." He waved goodbye as he jumped in his cab and I was left to try and figure out exactly what we had been talking about. Something about a mountain, as best I could recollect. But whatever it was, I promised myself I would try as hard as I could to pay closer attention to him.

He did say eight o'clock, didn't he? Why can't I focus?

5

Raising a Mountain

"Ah, Mr. Richard, so good to see you this morning! God has blessed us with another beautiful day in the Land of Egypt, has He not?"

I thought the cool, crisp morning air was exhilarating, and the air strikingly clear. "Yes, it is a beautiful day, Hordadef, and it's good to see you, too."

"Well then, we have a long day ahead of us, so we need to get started as soon as possible. It will not be easy describing how a mountain was built, but I will do my best, as I know our agreement is based on your complete satisfaction or my fee is in jeopardy. Is this not so, Mr. Richard?"

"Yes, that is our agreement."

"You are a tough customer, Mr. Richard, but I am a professional. So that is why Hordadef is not too concerned. Come, then. Let us get started. First we will take a ride in a competitor's cab."

Before I could ask, he had opened the door to a nearby cab and ushered me into the back seat. Then he opened the door to the front passenger's seat and got in, greeting the driver warmly in Arabic. He introduced the driver as Mr. Saleh al'Shafti.

"Good morning, sir, and welcome to Mr. Shafti's cab service. It is a pleasure to serve you today."

"Thank you," I responded.

He headed straight down the main thoroughfare, talking and laughing with Hordadef about a passenger he had picked up the previous day. We had driven several miles toward the Nile when he pulled the cab into a space in front of a small restaurant, where Hordadef got out and motioned for me to do the same. Hordadef paid Mr. Shafti, who then backed the cab out into the street and drove off.

I thought at first that Hordadef wanted to stop for breakfast, but he set off on foot back toward the Pyramid. We walked for quite a while in silence before he stopped and turned slowly in a circle, looking all around. "Tell me, Mr. Richard, what you see."

"What do I see where?"

"What do you see all around you?"

I considered the question for a minute, thinking that there had to be some trick to it, but decided that I would tell him exactly what was before my eyes.

"Well, there are restaurants, bakeries, houses, apartment buildings, gas stations, car repair shops, offices for professional services such as doctors and lawyers, furniture stores—all the things you would expect to find in a city, including lots of cars, trucks, and buses on the streets."

"That's right. And do you see how all of the buses are headed up to the pyramids on the plateau?"

"Yes, there is an almost endless stream of them."

"Precisely. And all around us are the people who live and work to support the tourists that the pyramids draw here. Now why do you suppose I have brought you here?"

"I really can't imagine."

"Do you agree that all of this activity has as its ultimate focus the Pyramid and the other pyramids on the plateau? And do you agree that everyone here is either working in support of the pyramids and the tourism they bring or providing the necessary services to others who do so?"

"Yes, I can appreciate that. The pyramids bring a lot of business here."

"This is true. But can you see with the eye of your imagination that what is all about you is not so different from what was here when the pyramids were being built? Thousands and thousands of people, all living and working in this same area, engaging in many of the exact same activities, all to support those working on the Pyramid. But instead of countless buses hauling tourists, an endless stream of stone and materials were headed up to the construction site, either along this same route or very close by. The people and things of the past, Mr. Richard, are really not much different from those of the present, are they?"

"I guess not, when you think about it that way."

"But there was one thing present then that no longer exists here, Mr. Richard. Do you know what that was?"

"I guess the stones."

"Yes, that too. But what is missing is the canal on which the great barges took supplies and construction materials up to the Pyramid. And instead of the sidewalks along the streets, there were towpaths used by the teams of oxen that pulled the barges."

We continued to walk as he talked.

"The barges brought stone here from several locations. The core blocks of rough limestone were cut nearby and hauled down to the river, where they were loaded onto the barges. The great blocks of granite used in the Pyramid were cut hundreds of miles upstream and loaded onto purpose-built barges for transport to this location. The fine-grained, white limestone used to face the Pyramid was cut across the River in the Turah Hills and also brought here by barge.

"The site for the Pyramid, acres and acres of ground, was cut down and almost perfectly leveled. The degree of error was almost microscopic. This in itself was no mean achievement. However, a core of the native rock was kept intact in the center to use as an initial reference point and guide in raising the Pyramid.

"The core blocks were brought directly up to the plateau, where they were laid and placed together, and the spaces between them filled with mortar to seal and keep them in place. The granite and facing limestone blocks, on the other hand, were first taken to a special stone working shop, located nearby, where they were cut with great saws and planers to exact sizes and measurements, and then finished by grinding and polishing. The shops used for this purpose lay in front of the Sphinx, and their ruins are still there. Most of the machines used for cutting and shaping the granite and fine limestone were driven by water, which came from the plateau above.

"The surfaces of the machine tools were made of very hard stone chips, specially selected and graded for their cutting characteristics and mounted in copper. These machines and the cutting tools were built and maintained by specially trained craftsmen.

"After the granite and fine limestone blocks were cut to size and specifications, they were brought into contact according to plan to ensure proper fit, as there was little or no opportunity for this once the stones were brought up to the Pyramid for setting. They had to be perfect and fit exactly as intended without fail; otherwise, construction of the Pyramid would be delayed and there was very little tolerance for such mistakes.

"Now, if there is a secret regarding the Pyramid, Mr. Richard, and I don't believe it to be so, it has to do with how it was built. It is really no secret at all, though, as the answer is water. Vast quantities of water were brought up to the plateau by means of sluiceways designed to raise water from the Nile River, twenty-four hours a day. Teams of oxen drove large pumps day and night without ceasing. You see, stone can only be moved and set during daylight, but water can be moved continuously, without regard to day or night. It was water that raised the barges that raised the stone. All quite efficient, do you not agree?"

"Yes, I hadn't thought of it before, but that seems very efficient. But how did they keep the water on the plateau?"

"We'll talk about that when we get up there. But see now how we are climbing up to the plateau. Do you know how the barges were made to climb?"

"It would have to be through a system of locks."

"Absolutely! And along this stretch the locks were massive. One of them was so big that it lifted the barges a full forty feet up the plateau. Again you see the efficiency of using water to do the work. It would have taken many long and backbreaking hours to drag the stones up here, and some of them were so large that quite likely it could not have been done. The stones for these locks were removed centuries ago, to help build the city of Cairo, but by then they had long been of no further purpose to the Pyramid."

We walked on up the plateau in silence, but once we reached the top and headed for the Pyramid, Hordadef grew animated.

"Mr. Richard, we are standing on a vast stone table that, during the construction we are speaking of, was enclosed by a stone wall to extend the canal's reach to the Pyramid itself. Imperfections in the rocky surface that permitted water to run off were sealed with mud. Barges laden with stone, mortar, and other building materials were pulled to one of several great graving docks cut into the rock to receive them. Once the barge was positioned over one of these docks, the gates were closed and the water pumped from it until the barge settled into the dock."

We looked down into one of the vast docks adjacent to the Pyramid. A second, identical dock was close by.

"Once the barge was firmly in the dock, smaller barges were brought alongside and the stones and building materials were offloaded onto them. These smaller barges were designed to fit a series of locks that were built like stairs into the eastern face of the Pyramid. Water was moved up the Pyramid almost constantly for the mortar, to operate the locks, and to move and set the stones in place, particularly the larger ones."

Hordadef walked to an area adjoining the eastern face of the Pyramid to the remains of what was officially called the mortuary temple. We stood on its diorite floor looking up. The Pyramid rose skyward before us.

"This was the access to the locks that the construction barges used to ascend the face of the Pyramid. Before each layer of the Pyramid was begun, the water reservoir for operating the locks was constructed. Then the lock for that level was built. The casing blocks for that level were moved into position along the face of the Pyramid and cemented into place. The entire space enclosed by the casing blocks was filled with water and the core blocks were brought up the locks on the construction barges, which were then floated into their approximate position on the layer under construction and ballasted down until they came to rest on the surface of the Pyramid. Drains built into the structure were opened and the water drained until the barges came to rest on the platform. After that, the blocks were taken off the barges and set into place using large lifting levers specially designed for the purpose. This process was repeated layer after layer until the top of the Pyramid narrowed too much to continue with the locks. At that point the levers were used to lift and swing the remaining blocks into position, and labor grew increasingly manual because of the constricted workspace."

It sounded so plausible, but my education forced me to ask what proof existed for his story.

"What proof do you require, Mr. Richard?"

"That such vast quantities of water were brought up the Pyramid in the fashion you described."

"Ah yes, proof. You are not convinced, then? Well, Mr. Richard, do you see what is before us here—a veritable mountain of stone, cut and set to perfection? Is this not proof that the Egyptians were master architects and builders to have designed and reared such a structure?"

"Of course. But you haven't offered any proof that they built it the way you described."

"So you concede that the Egyptians were a very gifted and creative people, yet you deny them these same traits when it comes to issues of technique and process? This is the illogical premise of your question: they were brilliant in some respects, but dull-witted in others."

He had me again. I had no response. Surely if the Egyptians could solve all of the problems associated with designing and building the Pyramid, they most assuredly were capable of solving the practical problems of bringing the stones and materials up the plateau and setting them in place. That they would haul such a vast quantity of material up there and set it in place by manual labor was indeed illogical. They were capable and efficient engineers, and they wouldn't have wasted so much labor when there was a better, easier way.

Hordadef was right. If there was a secret about building the Pyramid, it was that water was the means used to do it. And if there was backbreaking labor involved in the process, it was the oxen's, moving the water up the plateau and then a considerable way up the Pyramid itself until they could no longer be used because of the lack of working space. Then men were used, because at that point there was no alternative.

"I guess you're right, Hordadef. What you described is the easiest and most efficient way, and it is clear that the Egyptians were more than capable of it. I have to admit that until you told me what these great boat pits were used for, I had always believed, as have so many others, that they were built to hold imaginary boats. But your explanation makes much more sense."

I stared at him. How could a cab driver have such great knowledge?

"Who are you?"

"Excuse me, Mr. Richard? It's me, Hordadef. Are you okay? Is it getting too hot for you? Do you need more water?"

"No, I'm fine. But who are you and what do you really do?"

"I'm Hordadef, Mr. Richard, and as you well know I drive a cab."

"Did you go to the University?"

"Excuse me, Mr. Richard, the University? Me, a poor cab driver?" He threw his head back and laughed.

"Well, what did your father do?"

"He drove a cab, too."

"And his father? And his father before him . . . I suppose he also drove a cab?"

"Yes, a *caleche*. A horse-drawn one."

"So you come from a long line of cab drivers. Then how do you know so much about the Pyramid?"

"My father told me and his father told him."

"An oral history handed down through the generations?"

"A what?"

"An oral history. Your father told you, as his father told him, and so on and so forth. Isn't that how you came by your knowledge?"

"An oral history! I like that, Mr. Richard. Yes, that is what it was."

"Who were your ancestors?"

"Egyptians, Mr. Richard. All Egyptians."

"I mean what did they do? They couldn't all have been cab drivers."

"No, of course not. But I'm certain they were all men of simple means. Even the one they called the Greatest of Seers and the Keeper of the Secrets of Heaven and Earth."

"The what?!" Had I heard him correctly? Those were the honorifics bestowed on Egypt's greatest wise man, the legendary Imhotep! They echoed in my ears.

"They were all Egyptians of simple means, Mr. Richard, and they probably did whatever they could to sustain themselves and their families. The rest is oral history, as you call it. Knowledge handed down from generation to generation, passed along to me by my father as I am now passing it along to you, Mr. Richard."

"But why? Why me?"

"Because you want to know and are patient enough to learn. You also are the first visitor to come inquiring about the truths behind the legends of the things hidden in the Pyramid. No one else ever has, and that includes people who sought the services of my father, his father, his father, and so on. Besides, you and I have a contract, so I'm obligated to teach you. Is this not so, Mr. Richard?"

We laughed, but I knew that there was far more to this cab driver than he would ever reveal to me. I also knew it wasn't that important. Perhaps Hordadef and his family were nothing more than simple, unassuming people, and perhaps it was this that sustained them in preserving the great knowledge entrusted to them, by who knows who, when, or why. At that moment I didn't know what impressed me more: Hordadef or the Pyramid. They were both marvels to behold, and they even seemed to sustain one another in a mysterious way. Both were priceless legacies.

"Come, Mr. Richard. The stories for today are at an end. You should get some lunch and I need to see if I can pick up a couple of fares before this evening."

"I thought you were at my service for the entire day, under the terms of the daily rate?"

"Only so long as services are being rendered, Mr. Richard. And as I've just stated, the stories for today are at an end. If the services were satisfactory, then this concludes our business for today."

I smiled at him. "They were very satisfactory, Hordadef. Very satisfactory."

When we were ready to part, he told me that we would be getting a late start the following day, probably around nine o'clock at night, because that was the earliest appointment we could get to visit the Pyramid.

"Tomorrow night we will go into the Pyramid again and I will show you several of the spheres it holds and the knowledge that they preserve. It will be something you are likely never to forget, Mr. Richard, for they are a true wonder to behold."

6

The Celestial Spheres

The next day I got up early. After breakfast I went for a swim. In the afternoon I walked around the Pyramid, looking up at it and into the great boat pits that Hordadef had discussed with me the day before. My mind was elsewhere, though.

I couldn't help thinking about our pending visit to the Pyramid that night, and trying to imagine where the spheres were and what they looked like. But the more I tried to imagine them, the more doubt crept into my thoughts and the less I believed I would find anything even remotely like what I expected. Celestial spheres? If they were ever there, how could they possibly be there still? I had no doubts that Hordadef would show me something, but I began to fear that I would be disappointed. Then again, he did say that they were there and that they were a wonder to behold.

Hordadef's lessons were like no others that I had ever had and his knowledge of the Pyramid was truly breathtaking and unique in every respect. The things he had taught me about the significance of its location, its relationship to time and Earth measurements, and its relationship to Heaven were all truly impressive. And the terrestrial globe that he showed me, which was incorporated into its stones, was truly a marvel and a stunningly important feature of the Pyramid that must surely excite the imagination of everyone who is interested in Egypt and the pyramids. These were priceless lessons, though I had to admit that even the ancient Greeks knew some of these features of the Pyramid, particularly its relationship to the dimensions of the Earth. But not to this extent. And if I learned nothing more from him, he would still be the greatest teacher I had ever encountered and one of the wisest.

But celestial spheres in the Pyramid? This was surely a stretch, even for him.

People have been hacking into the Pyramid's stones for literally thousands of years, looking for the secrets and treasures that they believe must be hidden somewhere in its vast structure. But few if any of them have ever been rewarded for their efforts. Possibly something of value was hidden in it when it was first built, but whatever it was must surely be long gone. And yet people still come to it, to look upon it and study it, and believe that there has to be more, and that they could find it if only they could be clever enough and persistent enough. It is an impulse that even the most casual tourists feel while pushing on its stones, as countless others have done before, believing that one of them will give way and open up onto secret rooms and recesses that hold untold treasure and knowledge. And fame and fortune will smile upon them. Even the most studied and aloof scientist feels this, for it is all too human to want to believe such things.

And behind these thoughts is the most cynical of all, arising from man's innate greed and vanity: why else would someone build the Pyramid if not to hide something of great value?

In the face of such persistent attention and the almost ceaseless effort to pry open its secrets, how can there possibly be anything left undiscovered or hidden away in the Pyramid? And if something is there, how can Hordadef know about it and keep the secret to himself? Surely others would have seen him moving stones around, ducking into some secret passage, and his secret would have been discovered by now. To say nothing of his ancestors having had knowledge of such things, without it being found out long ago.

Such thoughts and questions persisted throughout the day. Somehow, though, I drew comfort from them, because I wanted to lower my expectations as much as possible to fit the reality that I was likely to encounter that night. There would probably be some pattern in one or more stones that could be construed to depict a sphere. Whatever it was, I wanted to be appreciative and not patronizing when Hordadef showed it to me. But no matter how many times I steered my thoughts to such practical conclusions, the romance and mystery of seeing something that no one had ever seen before would beckon my imagination on to new heights of fantasy.

And so the day proceeded until night finally came and I would finally learn exactly what was there. The moment had arrived.

I stepped out of the hotel courtyard and onto the streets. Hordadef was nowhere to be seen. At half past nine he still was not there and I began to think that something might have happened to him. Then at twenty minutes to ten he drove up and stopped the car in the middle of the road and told me to get in quickly. I jumped in and we sped up the road toward the plateau, barely slowing down for the guard station.

Within minutes we had parked the car and were walking hurriedly toward the Pyramid. We were late, but we still had an hour and fifteen minutes available for the visit. Hordadef spoke to the guards briefly and I saw him hand them some cash. Seconds later we hastened inside, bumping our heads repeatedly on the low ceiling of the Ascending Passage as we climbed up its confined ramp. Entering the Grand Gallery, we hardly broke stride and clambered up the wooden stairway built along its ramp. We cleared the Ante Chamber and then entered the King's Chamber. Hordadef leaned heavily against the wall and coughed deeply, struggling to catch his breath.

"Excuse me, Mr. Richard, but if this relationship is to continue you must consider giving up smoking. It is not good for you," he said, gasping for breath.

"Consider it done." We laughed. "What happened to you?"

"I had some notes and drawings that are crucial to tonight's lesson and it took me a while to find them. In any case, we still have time for the lesson if we hurry."

He moved to the center of the chamber and motioned for me to stand by him. As I did so, all my doubts of the afternoon came flooding back. *It will be some markings in the stones, just as I imagined*, I thought. I joined him and we faced the north wall.

"Now, Mr. Richard, do you remember the other day when we were at the ruins of the step pyramid in the desert near *Zawiyet el-Aryan* and I demonstrated for you how to measure altitude and azimuth?"

"I remember, but I am ashamed to admit that I wasn't paying as close attention as I should have, so maybe you could please refresh my memory?"

"Mr. Richard, Mr. Richard, did you waste your time and money like this when you were studying at the University? And did you beg the teacher's forgiveness and indulgence when you did? And I thought you were a good student. Tch, tch, tch! Are we paying attention now?"

"Yes."

"Altitude is angular measure above the horizon, on the northern or southern half of the celestial dome," he said, raising his right arm slowly from the level of the floor until it pointed directly over his head. Then he turned and faced the south wall and repeated the motion. "Azimuth, on the other hand, is angular measure along the level of the horizon, measured from north or south in an easterly or westerly direction." He moved his arm slowly along the level of the floor, first right and then left. (Figure #7) This is how the priests and mariners of old measured the locations of celestial bodies in the heavens and plotted their positions. It is an art older than the Pyramid itself and is still in use today among mariners in their practice of celestial navigation, though nowadays the priests probably have long forgotten it.

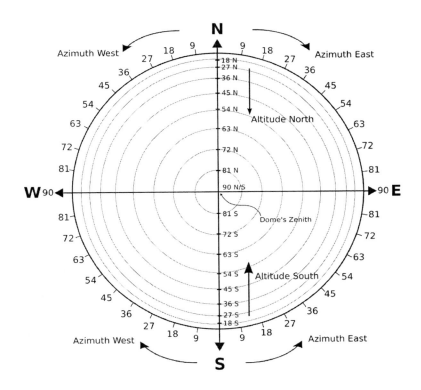

Reference Grid for Celestial Dome

Figure 7

"Now, Mr. Richard. Do you observe that there is a north wall, a south wall, an east wall, and a west wall?"

"Yes."

"Do you see that each wall is composed of five even courses of blocks and that the courses are all level with the floor?"

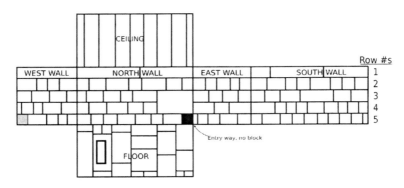

Note: Drawn from, Charles Piazzi Smyth, Our Inheritance in the Great Pyramid;
2nd Edition, 1877, Plate XIV. The 3rd row of the south wall was modified,
per the 4th edition, 1880, p. 170; based on the observation
of Flinders Petrie as concurred in by C.P. Smyth.

Arrangement of Blocks in the King's Chamber

Figure 8

"Yes."

"And can you see that whoever designed and built this chamber did so with an extraordinary attention to detail, cutting the stones and setting them with great precision, even though all of the stones are granite and each of them weighs many tons?"

"Yes."

"Look around you at the various blocks and observe that some are much larger than others, but that all were cut and placed with this same level of care. Is it not apparent that whoever designed and built this chamber could have cut the stones to any size and shape, and set them in any manner desired, such was the level of their skill and artistry?"

"Yes. It is all very impressive."

"Indeed it is, but they chose to cut and set them in this specific manner, which as you will see had purpose. There is a pattern and meaning in the number and setting of the stones, Mr. Richard. Everything was done by design, with nothing left to chance. Now then. Please tell me how many blocks you see in the ceiling."

"There are 9."

"That is correct. Here is a table showing the numbers of blocks in each row on each wall. You will note that each wall has a number of blocks that is divisible by 9, with the exception of the west wall. However, there is a block along the floor of the west wall that is different than the others, both with respect to how it is set and the precision with which it is cut. Several people who have studied this chamber in great detail observed this feature, which was done by design so that the stone could be counted or omitted as necessary to the function at hand. And for this purpose, Mr. Richard, the stone is not counted and the west wall can be presumed to have 18 blocks, which is divisible by 9. You counted 9 blocks in the ceiling. Are we agreed?"

I stared at the table, then looked up at the ceiling again. "Agreed."

	North	East	South	West
1st Row	2	1	3	1
2nd Row	7	5	8	4
3rd Row	6	4	6	4
4th Row	5	3	9	5
5th Row	7	5	10	5
Total	27	18	36	19

Number of Blocks in Each Wall by Row
Table 1

"The Pyramid's designers intended for the number 9 to be a factor, Mr. Richard. Moreover, there are 9 gods of the Heliopolitan Ennead: Atum Re, Shu, Tefnut, Geb, Nut, Horus (in Osiris's place), Seth, Isis, and Nephthys. These gods set sail across the heavens on the Boat of Millions of Years at the beginning of time and will circle the Earth until the end of time. The 9 blocks above us symbolize the bottom of this boat.

"However, it is as a factor that the number 9 concerns us for the moment." He handed me another sheet of paper. "This table, Mr. Richard, multiplies the number of blocks in each row by the number 9. Do you see this?"

"Yes."

	North Altitude	East Azimuth	South Altitude	West Azimuth
1st Row	18	9	27	9
2nd Row	63	45	72	36
3rd Row	54	36	54	36
4th Row	45	27	81	45
5th Row	63	45	90	45

Angular Coordinates in Degrees
Table 2

"Okay, then. This table gives us altitude and azimuth points that can be plotted on a sphere or a dome, which is half a sphere. For example, in the 3rd row there are 4 points: (54N, 36 E), (54N, 36W), (54S, 36E), and (54S, 36W). The first point, (54N, 36E), lies 54º above the floor or horizon." He raised his arm, pointing north. "And 36º to the right or east along the horizon." He swung his upraised arm right. "Do you see how the point can be plotted in this manner?"

"Yes, but I don't see the sphere."

"Would you agree that if we did this outside while looking up at the heavens, this point would lie in a particular location in the heavens? And do you also agree that the heavens are perceived as a sphere or dome, from our perspective on Earth?"

"Yes."

"Well, then, it is the same thing. The points that derive from the blocks in the walls of the chamber can all be plotted and will appear to us as if they were plotted on the sphere of the heavens. Angles of altitude and azimuth are the measures used for determining the celestial coordinates of the stars and planets of the heavens. And plots of their coordinates can be created by projecting them onto a flat surface, using the circle with the quartering cross as a grid. This grid is so fundamental to the practice of astronomy that to this day it is used as the symbol for the Earth. Do you understand?"

He handed me another piece of paper depicting a circle marked off with degrees of altitude and azimuth—the cross in a circle—which I stared at for several minutes.

"Yes," I replied. Suddenly it all became clear to me and I saw how each row of blocks could define points on a celestial sphere. *How clever! How very clever! But what is on the spheres?* Hordadef did not pause long enough for me to ask aloud.

"The meaning of this room, Mr. Richard, begins in number, proceeds to geometry through the practice of astronomy, which in turn produces symbols. However, it is religion that allows us to interpret the symbols and learn their message.

"Please, sit down," he said, and we both sat on the floor of the chamber. "Now, Mr. Richard, at the risk of repeating myself I cannot overstate that there is only One God and that He is ultimately beyond man's ability to fully understand or comprehend. However, He has an infinite number of divine attributes that may be talked about and examined, all in an effort to gain an understanding and knowledge of Him, however imperfect the effort may be. These various attributes were apportioned among the gods and goddesses that the ancient Egyptians named and assigned identities and features to for this purpose. Done right, this can lead man closer to God; done wrong, it can lead to idolatry. The ancient Egyptians recognized this and struggled with it for centuries, but in the end they succumbed to idolatry and their civilization was swept away.

"Tonight we will speak of the gods and their sacred things, but know that it is really of the One God. The five rows each define a separate sphere on which are depicted certain objects or information. The 1st, 3rd, and 5th rows depict symmetrical objects or symbols, which, when considered by themselves or in combination with those from the other two, are profoundly sacred. And there is a sequence to them that describes how God created the universe. The 2nd and 4th rows depict asymmetrical patterns that are important to the knowledge incorporated into the Pyramid, but we will speak of them at another time."

He looked at me for a moment. "If I'm going too fast, please stop me."

"I will, but I'm okay so far."

"And we are paying attention, are we not?"

"Yes, yes, of course."

"Good! Now all of the points plotted can be connected directly with one another with straight or diagonal lines, or with a circle. This is what creates the objects. Then by removing some of these lines and emphasizing others, or by making certain minimal but logical additions, the meaning of the symbols is made clearer. As you can imagine, the designer and author of these objects faced an overriding need for economy of expression because of the limited number of spheres, so only those objects considered most important were used. And some of the objects were specifically designed to serve multiple functions and to be used on other spheres. You should also understand that there is some distortion along the edges in the drawings of the objects that I am going to show you, because they are done on a flat surface, whereas the actual objects were designed for viewing on the underside of a sphere or a dome."

He handed me a piece of paper on which several objects were drawn. "This is the 1st sphere," he said, and I looked on it intently as he continued.

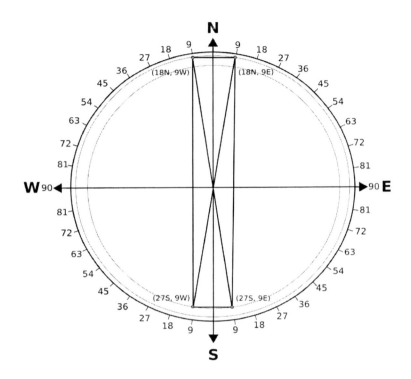

1st Celestial Sphere Symbols

Figure 9

"The drawing depicts the twin-ringed orb of Atum Re, the creator god. Atum Re was the first god created by Ptah. Ptah called forth to Atum Re, who was floating listlessly in the dark depths of the abyss. In response, Atum Re awoke, found awareness, and broke free of a great serpent that had imprisoned him in its coils. This great serpent is the space between the inner and outer circles of the symbol of Atum Re in the 1st row's drawings, and represents time without end, as the serpent forever chases its tail throughout the ages. Atum Re then searched about for something to cling to or stand on and found the primeval perch or pillar, which is the second object depicted in the drawing. From atop this perch, Atum Re called forth the names and destinies of all things. This was the beginning of what the Egyptians called *Tep Zepi*, or the First Time.

"Also note that the pillar extends some 9° to either side of the center dividing line, and is crossed diagonally in both directions. This is approximately the same width as the band of the ecliptic (the apparent path of the Sun) that circles the Earth, and in which the Sun, the Moon, and the five planets of Mercury, Venus, Mars, Jupiter, and Saturn all move in their apparent path around the Earth. The Sun moves down the center line, while the Moon and planets move in sinuous motions within the band, but never beyond its limits." (Appendix 3)

He handed me another drawing (Figure #10). It had the orb of Atum Re and the rectangle removed from it, leaving only the diagonals, which had the appearance of two swords opposed to one another, tip to tip. Hordadef had labeled the drawing Swords of Divine Fire.

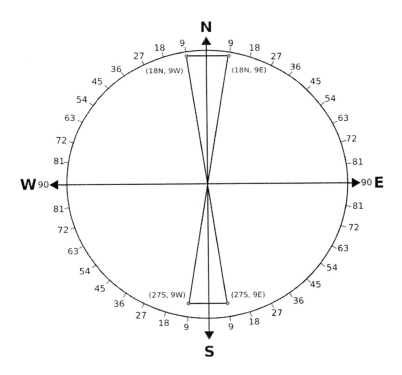

Swords of Divine Fire

Figure 10

"Remember this drawing," he said, "because we will use it later in conjunction with the objects from several of the other spheres."

The next drawing was of a rectangle within a circle (Figure #11). The rectangle was diagonally divided into a series of mer triangles (36º–54º–90º). The next drawing showed the same figures, but two other radii had been added, which along with the several already present divided the circle into five equal arcs, each of 72º (Figure #12). The drawing following this one cross-connected the five points of the 72º arcs, creating a stunning pattern (Figure #13), which was labeled The Crossed Arrows of Neith, Mother of the Gods. The arrows were obvious, but so was the fact that they formed a five-pointed star. Hordadef referred to this final drawing to point out that this star was not only the insignia of the Pythagorean societies, but also the insignia of the Egyptian priests who watched and studied the heavens—Egypt's astronomers.

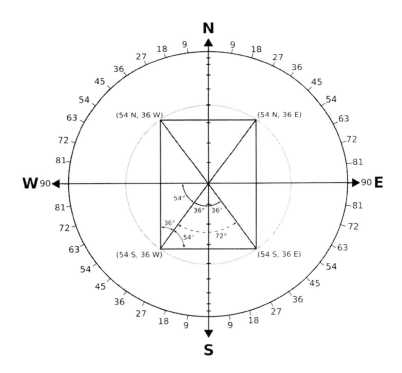

2nd Celestial Sphere Symbols
(mer triangles)
Figure 11

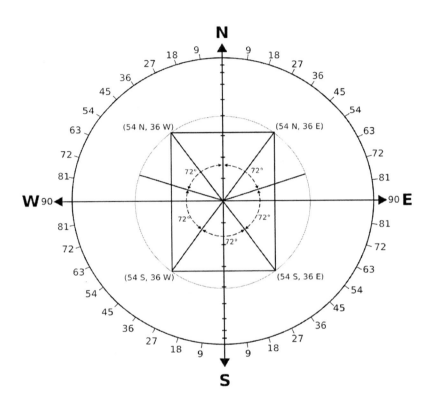

The Circle from 2nd Sphere Divided into 72° Segments

Figure 12

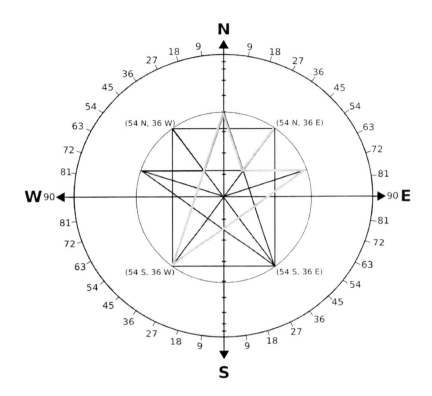

Crossed Arrows of Neith
Mother of the Gods
Figure 13

"This star, Mr. Richard, depicts the golden mean through the intersections of its five lines. Each of these lines creates the proportion of the golden mean; that is, the length of each line is to the larger bisected portion as the larger portion is to the smaller. Also, the *mer* triangle from which the star is composed, with its unique angular and linear relationships, enabled the Egyptians to figure the trigonometric functions for the acute angles of any right triangle. To the ancients, the logic inherent in the *mer* triangle's form and number was the underlying order of the universe, and they believed that it was used by God to delineate both Heaven and Earth. The five-pointed star, then, was a practical device that could be used for calculating a number of geometric and trigonometric relationships.

"Neith, the mother of the gods and the most ancient goddess, gave birth to all of the lesser gods. Atum Re named them and assigned them their positions in the heavens as stars, where they were affixed to the invisible guide wires on which they swing in eternal motion around the Great Seat of Ptah to this day. Once all of the stars of the lesser gods were arrayed in their positions, God set the universe in motion and time began.

"The 5th row, Mr. Richard, generated these symbols." He handed me another series of drawings. I looked at the first one for a moment, noting that the symbols were all located in the upper part of the circle (Figure # 14).

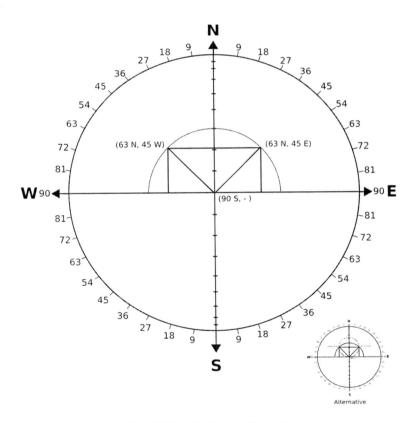

The 3rd Celestial Sphere Symbols

Figure 14

"The first alternative drawing shows awareness emerging from the lotus of the god Nefertum (Figure #15). This next one is of Sokar, Lord of Eternity, in his egg at the very depths of the underworld that the Sun travels through each night, and that every soul passes through after death (Figure #16). Sokar is the god of resurrection and reincarnation. This one is the cup of creation that God used to mix the elements of the universe (Figure #17). It was also used to create all mortal life, and if we combine the swords from the symbols of the 1st row with the triangular cup from the symbols of the 5th row, we get this drawing (Figure #18). It shows the divine fire of God and mortal elements of the universe being mixed together in the cup of creation to create mortal life. It is the moment written of in Plato's Timaeus:

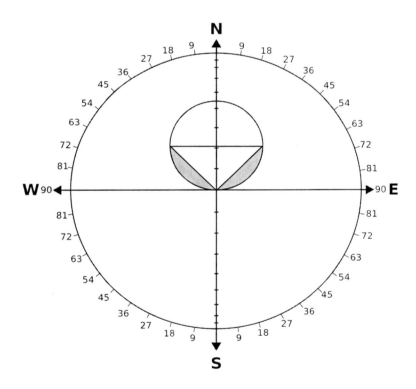

Nefertum Emerges from the Lotus

Figure 15

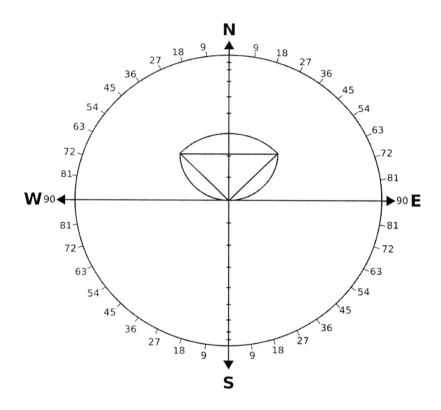

The Luminescent Egg of Sokar

Figure 16

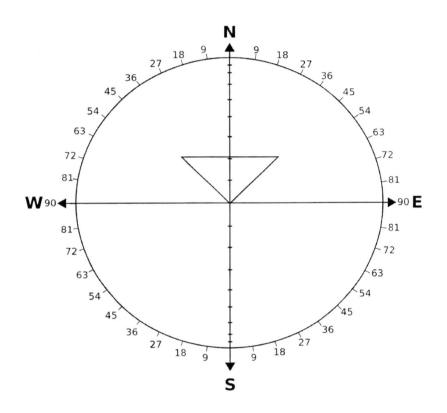

God's Cup of Creation

Figure 17

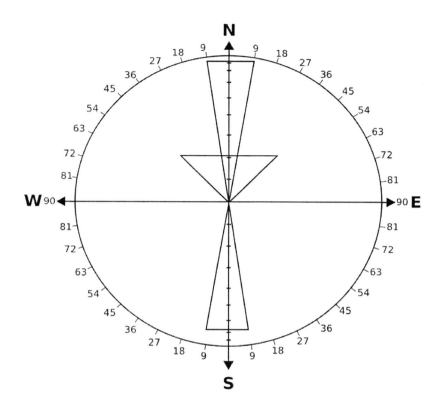

Creation of Mortal Life
(Symbols Combined)
Figure 18

"I will myself sow the seed ... Thus He spake, and once more into the cup in which he had previously mingled the soul of the universe, He poured the remains of the elements and mingled them in much the same manner ..."

"The final drawing combines several previous drawings (Figure #19). It is life continuing until the end of time, striving toward the perfection that was reserved to the lesser gods by God Himself.

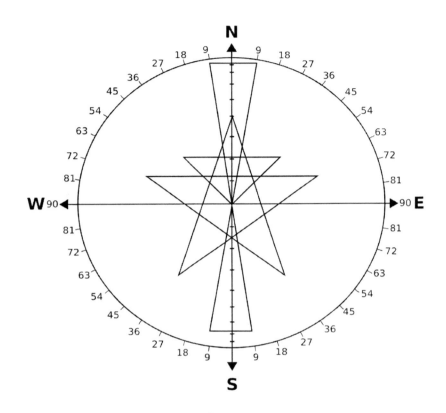

Growing Toward Perfection
(Symbols Combined)
Figure 19

"The symbols generated by these three rows of stones undoubtedly can be manipulated to produce others, as that is the nature of such things. They embody both form and number, both inherent in the nature of the universe, as God intended in its design. Symbols merge, combine, and remerge, each provoking thought and understanding of the mysteries of God in the heart and soul of man. There is an ordered logic to them, as the first row deals with the beginning of the universe, continues with the laying out of the heavens and the creation of the lesser gods in the third row, and concludes with the creation of mortal life in the fifth row. Collectively, they speak of the greatest mysteries of life—how and why each began, and how and why it yet sustains itself. They convey as much knowledge and understanding of these things as is permitted man; more than this will forever remain hidden from him and is known only by God."

I intently inspected the second to last drawing he had handed me. The simplicity of its lines and form and the clarity of its message were at once direct and strikingly beautiful. I was mesmerized. I wanted to go back through each of the drawings again, but Hordadef reached over and turned them all face down.

"Listen to me, Mr. Richard. These things that I have shown you, these things of God, are not, properly speaking, secrets. They are knowledge that all men should strive to attain. Here in the deepest recesses of the Pyramid, permanently memorialized in these stones, are what its builders felt to be some of the most important things worth preserving in the very limited space available to them. The things that are recorded here constitute the greatest knowledge: who and what we are and our relationship with God and the universe He created. Take them, remember them, learn from them, and seek to understand them. There is no greater task that a man can set himself in this world.

"The hour is late, Mr. Richard. We must go."

We rose and left the Pyramid in silence.

As Hordadef pulled the cab up to the hotel, I thanked him for the lesson and we said goodnight. He told me he would pick me up around ten o'clock the next morning and drove off. I walked to my room almost in a daze, expecting that my thoughts of what I had seen and learned that night would keep me awake. I was wrong. Exhausted, I fell asleep in minutes.

7

The Key to the Stars

So the ancient legends of the Jews and the Arabs might be true after all!

The Pyramid contained terrestrial globes and celestial spheres . . . or at least what Hordadef had shown me so far were spheres of a sort. Maybe cosmic spheres was a more apt description of them than celestial spheres. In any case, they clearly touched on matters regarding God and Heaven, and there were more spheres to be revealed. And how intriguing it was that they were based on numbers, the universal language of Heaven, and geometry, the sacred science.

I looked at the drawings of the spheres Hordadef had given me the night before and was impressed with the designs on them. The idea crossed my mind that the designs or symbols drawn from the peculiar arrangement of the blocks in the King's Chamber might be a mere coincidence. But the drawings from the 1st and 3rd rows were particularly impressive and it was hard to believe that they could be accidental.

The drawing from the 5th row was a little less convincing in this regard. But in some respects the symbols drawn from it were the most intriguing of all, as they were related to some of Egypt's oldest and most obscure gods. In fact, the gods whose symbols were depicted in every one of the drawings, Atum Re, Neith, Sokar, and Nefertum—the latter being the god born of the opening lotus—were all associated with the beginning of the universe and of life on Earth and its continuity. This seemed too unlikely a coincidence. As Hordadef had said, there was a story line or narrative that easily and naturally played out when one reviewed them.

I wanted to find fault with them, a reason not to believe. But the more I tried, the more I was drawn to them. Hordadef was right. They did invoke thoughts about God and life. The more I contemplated them, the deeper were my thoughts in this regard. Perhaps that was by design. If so, whoever built the King's Chamber was a genius without equal.

I wanted to continue with my thoughts, but I needed to get going if I was to meet Hordadef at ten o'clock as agreed. I showered, dressed, and headed for the restaurant to grab a quick bite. As I sat eating my breakfast, I stared out the window at the Pyramid, thinking what a masterpiece it really was. The spheres and the symbols on them that Hordadef had shown me only deepened my appreciation for it. I looked at my watch. It was ten past ten.

Moments later I was on the street, where Hordadef was laughing and joking with several other cab drivers. We saw each other almost at the same time.

"Ah, good morning, Mr. Richard," he greeted me loudly. "And how are you on this fine day in the Land of Egypt? I hope you are well rested and ready for another day of Hordadef's stories."

"Good morning to you, Hordadef. I am indeed well. And, as always, it is a pleasure to see you and I look forward to your stories."

"A pleasure, Mr. Richard? Perhaps your satisfaction with my services has grown to the point where you may want to demonstrate it in the form of a larger tip?" He laughed out loud.

"We'll see," I said. "We'll see."

"Then let us be off for the day's appointments, for I haven't a minute to lose if I am to prove to you that I deserve a very generous tip."

Hordadef grabbed two large bottles of water from his car and waved goodbye to his colleagues, and we headed up toward the plateau and pyramids. I hadn't discussed the day's itinerary with him, but it made sense that we were going where I could question him about the spheres and drawings.

I paid our admission fees at the guard station and we walked up the road. I asked Hordadef why the knowledge of the spheres had been lost and he said it hadn't, as he obviously knew about it. But that wasn't what I meant. I asked several more times, but each time he claimed that the knowledge had never really been lost, just overlooked or ignored with the passing of time until it appeared lost, because men no longer appreciated the Pyramid for what it really was.

Hordadef asked if I was reading the note he gave me on the first night of our lessons. I was embarrassed. I had almost forgotten about it. He must have noticed my awkwardness because he dropped the matter. So I asked if it could have been only a coincidence that the stones of the King's Chamber had generated the symbols on the spheres.

"A coincidence?"

"Yes. You know. Just a random, chance event or series of events."

"Let me ask you this, Mr. Richard. Where did the legends come from that led to your trip to Egypt? Was it coincidence that these legends were borne out by the spheres and their drawings? Did you not find what the legends spoke of and what you were looking for?"

"No, that's not what I mean. Can you take any room with regular rows of blocks along its walls and generate spheres and drawings?"

"I suppose it's possible. But you're forgetting that the rows and the numbers of blocks in each row in the King's Chamber were factors of the number 9, which, as I showed you, was also designed into the chamber. If you could find another similar chamber, then, yes, it could produce drawings, but not without some inherent logic to the arrangement and number of blocks built into its walls. Otherwise the drawings it would produce would be incoherent. And as you saw from the drawings that I showed you, there was logic to them, both individually and collectively. This was no coincidence, Mr. Richard. It was all done by design."

"Yes, I agree, but it all seems a little too perfect."

"So what do you want to believe? That this is all the stuff of stories made up by Hordadef? Stories to entertain, but of little substance? Is this what you want to believe?"

"No, not at all. I was just wondering."

"You know what I think, Mr. Richard? You're like many modern people: well educated, long on formal knowledge, but so overly prideful in your ability to push the limits of that knowledge that you refuse to accept anything unless you can prove it for yourself beyond a doubt. That is called arrogance, Mr. Richard, as it dismisses all efforts but your own and considers them to be of dubious value and reliability. The people of knowledge who lived before us were not all fools and simpletons. Some of them were as smart as you or I, and maybe much more so. Their words deserve deference and credibility until they are unequivocally demonstrated to be in error, and not treated as suspect until you can satisfy yourself as to their accuracy. Is this not so, Mr. Richard? Would you yourself not prefer to be treated in this manner by future generations?"

He had me again. So much of modern scholarship does indeed reject the voices of the past unless their words can be shown to be accurate by modern standards of proof. There is no other word for it but arrogance. Still, I didn't know what to think about the spheres and their drawings. I supposed I had no other choice but to accept them, as their existence had been the stuff of legend and now those legends stood revealed as truth through Hordadef's teachings and guidance. Perhaps the best thing to do was to accept what they were until it could be demonstrated otherwise, as Hordadef suggested.

So engrossed had I been in our conversation that I barely noticed we had passed from the noisy crowds of people that surrounded the Pyramid to the relative quiet and tranquility of the paths separating the rows of *mastabas*, or burial structures, that lay between the Pyramid and the village below. As we walked along I looked at the structures and wondered who was buried there and what their lives had been like.

"It's funny, is it not, Mr. Richard? Here are all of these people who once walked the Earth, and undoubtedly disagreed with and fought with one another over things trivial and momentous. Yet here they are at rest in perfect order and harmony for all eternity. Makes you wonder if most of the things we concern ourselves with day to day are an utter waste of time, when this is what all things lead to. Perhaps we would be better advised to learn to appreciate the journey of life and prepare ourselves for what lies beyond."

"Yes, you're right. I was just trying to imagine who these people were and how they lived, but none of that truly matters now, does it? And who knows? Maybe some of our respective ancient ancestors several thousand years ago were engaged in the exact same activities as you and I on this exact same spot, wondering these exact same things about the dead who lie here? Now there's a thought!"

"Indeed, Mr. Richard, except that I am certain your ancient ancestor was probably far more generous toward mine for his services than you are toward me."

"Excuse me?"

We both laughed as we cleared the rows of *mastabas* and came to a bluff overlooking the Sphinx. We paused briefly to rest and then continued on. Several minutes later we were walking around the Sphinx with hundreds of other tourists. Hordadef asked if I knew the significance of the Sphinx and I told him that it was part of Pharaoh Khafre's pyramid complex and had been built in his likeness. Khafre was the builder of the second great pyramid on the plateau of Giza.

"More likely," he said, staring up at the face of the great sculpture, "Khafre used the image of the Sphinx on his statues. The Sphinx is from an era many thousands of years earlier than Khafre's reign and was built to memorialize an event that has earned the sculpture an enduring epithet, the Father of Terrors. The Sphinx was carved in imitation of the constellation Leo, which is one of the signs of the zodiac, because it was during the last days of the Age of Leo that the great Flood occurred, one of the things spoken of in the legends you are studying. The catastrophe occurred when "the Heart of the Lion reached the first minute of the Head of Cancer," according to Ibrahim Ebn Wasuff Shah, the Arab historian, or approximately 10,500 years ago. This is what the Sphinx signifies, Mr. Richard. It is a moment in time that man should never forget.

"Look at the base of the Sphinx and all along the walls of the embayment that it sits in. Do you not see the deep marks of water erosion everywhere, marks that could only have been made after the Sphinx was carved out of the surrounding rock? And yet, as you see, there is no water today, nor has there been any substantial amount in the area for eons. Certainly nothing that could account for this type of wear."

I had heard this theory before, but I knew that most Egyptologists simply ignored it. Its ramifications were too unsettling and too difficult to fit into accepted chronologies. Egyptologists offered no countervailing theories of their own; they only met it with their collective silence. I had to admit that I was largely in this same camp, as I too found it difficult to accept that the Sphinx might be a relic from a far earlier age. Such a conclusion would not only up-end established Egyptology, it would force a rethinking of the entire history of the world. And that was a thought much too difficult to comprehend. Its ramifications went far beyond Egyptology and history—they went to the very meaning of man's existence on Earth and his relationship with God.

Here I was, possibly on the verge of learning that the Flood, arguably the most significant part of the ancient legends concerning the Pyramid, might also be true, thus providing a sound basis in fact for my thesis. And I found myself totally unnerved by the prospect. Why?

All of us have been taught to believe that the history of mankind is one of ever-increasing progress, interrupted of course by brief setbacks, but ultimately an upward movement toward higher and higher levels of civilization, sophistication, and knowledge. We have journeyed from primitive stone-age creatures, with lives only marginally different from animals, to rudimentary civilization, to today's complex and sophisticated culture. A gradual and orderly progress. The belief in such continuous progress, though interrupted at times, is an enduring and comforting one because we need it to be so. It is incomprehensible to us that it could all be destroyed in an instant, and that we could be thrown back down the ladder that we climbed so arduously and patiently to reach our present level of civilization. Because we cannot accept it happening to us, we refuse to believe that it could have happened in the past to our ancestors. The Flood is a myth, a fanciful story and nothing more, we tell ourselves. How could it possibly be otherwise?

Yet I was now staring at possible evidence of such an event. I didn't say anything to Hordadef because I couldn't.

"Can you imagine what the Sphinx has been witness to, Mr. Richard? Can you imagine the stories it could tell?"

I shook my head. It was beyond my comprehension. Far better, I thought, that I believed the Sphinx was carved in Pharaoh Khafre's image to satisfy his vanity. The alternative was too unsettling.

"Come, Mr. Richard. We need to return to the Pyramid."

I trundled off behind him, back up the path we had just traveled down. Each step of the way, my fear of what lay in store on the plateau grew. I wanted to know the truth, but the prospect raised a feeling of dread in me. These secrets had rested in obscurity for countless centuries and mankind was apparently none the worse off for not knowing. Would things be different if the truth was known and we were forced to confront the reality? Would we reflect on our present attitude and conduct in the light of the newfound knowledge, and humble ourselves before forces larger than we are? Or would we recoil in horror at the revelation, and feel so threatened that we would close our minds to it as quickly as possible, lest it undermine our deep, abiding faith in our own devices to shape and control our destiny?

Should I continue to pursue the truth or just leave it shrouded in the obscurity where I found it? I would soon know.

We passed along the east side of the Pyramid and continued on to the north face, stopping at some distance away to avoid the crowds. We drank some water to refresh ourselves. Even though the temperature was fairly mild, walking around in the heat of the full sun and the dryness of the desert taxed both of us.

Hordadef stood silently for several minutes, either trying to shake off the effects of our walk or to prepare himself for what he was about to say.

* * *

"Okay then, Mr. Richard. You should know several more things about the Pyramid before we return to the King's Chamber tonight. The Descending Passage that gives access to its interior runs for a considerable distance through the body of the Pyramid and continues on through the bedrock under it. Altogether it is several hundred feet long and is a wonder in its own right for its accuracy. Throughout its length its downward direction of travel is almost perfectly true along an angle of some $26.5°$. The variances of the floor, ceiling, and walls are on the order of $+1/4$ of an inch from true, while closer to the opening of the passageway the variance is less than $+1/50$ of an inch. In other words, it is almost perfectly straight.

"Scientists and explorers of the Pyramid, such as Piazzi Smyth, Flinders Petrie, and Richard Anthony Proctor, all marveled at its accuracy but wondered why it wasn't directed at the North celestial pole. The builders certainly were well aware of the direction of true north, and they had the technical knowledge to aim it precisely wherever they wanted. So the question arises, what did they aim it toward? Several scientists theorized that it had been aimed at Alpha Draconis, when that star was polar or circumpolar several thousand years ago. But the dates when this star was in a position to shine down the passageway were inconsistent with the generally accepted chronology for the Pyramid's construction. So the mystery persisted.

"One heavenly object shone directly down the passage when it was circumpolar. Your legends speak of it, Mr. Richard. Abu Zeyd al Balkhy quotes an ancient inscription, which stated that the Pyramid was built 'when the Lyre was in Cancer.' In other words, it was built when the Lyre or, more to the point, when one of its stars was circumpolar during the Age of Cancer. Now by our modern calculations, the constellation of Lyre could not have been anywhere near polar or circumpolar when the Earth was in the Age of Cancer, because the North celestial pole at the time was well past that location and aiming at a fairly inconspicuous section of the heavens.

"However, let us trust to the ancients for the moment and agree that they must have believed it was focused on a star in the Lyre, when the Age of Leo was ending and that of Cancer was beginning. If that were indeed the case, the star that the Descending Passage was aimed toward is one of the brightest in the northern heavens—Vega. In fact, Mr. Richard, it was Vega that the shaft was precisely aimed toward and al Balkhy's words are entirely accurate. Your legends have proved accurate once more.

"But I must defer further explanation on this particular point for the time being, as it is a subject best left to another lesson. Suffice it to say for the moment, though, that the shaft's alignment with Vega preserves the memory of the time of the Flood. It did in fact occur 'when the Lyre was in Cancer.' This is also consistent with the legends surrounding the Sphinx that maintain the Flood occurred 'when the Heart of the Lion would reach the first minute of the Head of Cancer.'

"The Descending Passage's alignment on Vega is the key to producing tables and charts of the stars as they appeared at the time of the Pyramid's construction. With this line defined and anchored to the North celestial pole, which was near Vega, and knowing the Great Age of the Zodiac, which was in the closing years of Leo, you can plot all the stars in the heavens in their earlier positions by taking their present positions and correcting them for the change to the location of the North celestial pole. This is not as complicated as it seems. One of the few things that truly changes in the heavens with respect to the orientation of the Earth is the location of the North celestial pole. If you know where the pole used to be at a particular time, you can reconstruct the heavens as they appeared. You have the key to the stars."

I wanted to question him, but once again his level of knowledge easily surpassed mine and I was unable to find the words. I basically grasped the concept of the North celestial pole moving in a slow circle around Ptah, or the North ecliptic pole. But how could it be in one location at the end of the Age of Leo and the beginning of the Age of Cancer and then move without the ages changing, too? That thought puzzled me. Then again, he did say that he had further things to say on the matter.

My earlier misgivings about finding proof of the Flood resurfaced, but they paled in significance for the time being as my mind focused on the particulars of Hordadef's statements. Unable to formulate or ask any questions, I kept silent. We remained there several minutes without talking, when suddenly he said we should probably get something to eat and prepare for our visit to the Pyramid later that evening.

"I know a little restaurant in Mena Village where we can get some excellent chicken *shawarmas* and *baba ganoj*. Would you like to join me?"

"I would be honored," I said, and we headed back down the road to his cab.

8

Death of Osiris and the Destruction of the Earth

The Giza Café was not far from the Pyramid but clearly off the regular tourist route. The late-afternoon streets were dusty, quiet, and devoid of traffic. As Hordadef parked the cab, I noticed a few children staring at us from the shadows of nearby buildings. I waved to them and they waved right back and smiled.

The café was nondescript and small, and from the outside appeared dark. When we entered, however, several lights and overhead fans came on. That seemed to signal that the restaurant's afternoon slumber was over and it was time to prepare for the evening's cooler temperatures and quickening pace of activity.

An elderly woman emerged from a doorway behind the counter and welcomed Hordadef warmly. He returned her greeting and they chatted in animated Arabic, sometimes laughing loudly. Then she looked at me and Hordadef apologized in English for not having introduced me.

"Mr. Richard, this is Kadija, the owner of this fine establishment. She says to tell you that you are very welcome here."

She smiled broadly at me and I at her, asking Hordadef to tell her that it was my pleasure to be here. They talked again in Arabic before she left through the doorway.

Hordadef steered us to a table and asked if I minded if he smoked. I said no and he lit a cigarette. A minute later Kadija reappeared and placed several bottles of water in front of us, along with napkins, knives, and forks. She returned to the kitchen.

"You have not said much about the evidence I showed you earlier today about the Flood, Mr. Richard. Either you have accepted all of it without question or are overwhelmed. We have been working together long enough now that I believe I can tell when you are overwhelmed or confused. Am I correct?"

"Somewhat correct. I have some questions about your earlier statements, but I decided to hold off asking them until I've heard the entire story, which you indicated you would tell me later. I've had doubts about whether I really want to know the truth about the Flood. I mean, I want to know, but part of me recoils at the ramifications of it. It's just inconceivable that the Earth could be destroyed and life, or most of it, utterly extinguished in an instant. How could it have happened?"

"Your fears are reasonable and your tentativeness in the face of the truth is entirely understandable," he said. "It shows that you have been thinking about the Flood the way that it should be thought of: the greatest catastrophe to ever befall man and a monstrous terror without comparison. Truly it is an event that should only be approached with great dread and fear."

"It's not fear, Hordadef. Just doubt that such knowledge could benefit me or anyone else. If it's something that happened and could happen again, and there's nothing anyone can do to stop it, then what is the point of knowing?"

"If you didn't know you were going to die one day, would you be better off or not?"

"That's not a fair comparison. Everyone knows they're going to die one day and that there is nothing anyone can do to stop it. But knowledge of the Flood is quite another matter. Of what possible benefit to people would knowledge of such a catastrophe be, and why should people know and worry about something that may never occur again? Wouldn't everyone be better off believing that it was all a myth?"

"Good questions, but let me ask you one first. Then most probably you will find the answers to your own questions. If people knew that ten years from this very date it would happen again, do you think they would behave differently?"

I stared at him while my mind stumbled again and again, trying to regain its equilibrium to respond. But I could think of no other response than to agree. "Yes, of course, most of them would behave differently. They would probably be more charitable and kinder toward their fellow man, and less enamored of material things, knowing that everyone faced imminent death on a certain date."

"And what of God? Would they humble themselves before Him and strive to lead better lives?"

"Yes."

"Then, Mr. Richard, I think you've answered your questions and resolved your doubts, have you not?"

I stared down at the table before responding. "Yes."

"But while this knowledge would benefit most men, it would not benefit all," he continued. "There will always be those who cannot or will not accept the truth. For them, nothing further can be done and they will invariably give in to their base appetites and their worst natures."

I was about to agree when Kadija brought our food. Hordadef engaged her in conversation while I began to eat. When more customers came in and Kadija turned to assist them, Hordadef ate his dinner. The rest of our dinner conversation was small talk. We left the restaurant thirty minutes later.

Darkness had settled over the village and the streets had come alive with people and cars. While getting to the café had proved fairly easy, getting back to the main street was a struggle. After much horn blaring and sudden braking, and a few death-defying swerves, we were back on the road leading to the plateau. Hordadef honked and waved to the security guards as we headed up to the plateau. We parked and made for the Pyramid once more.

* * *

As we entered the King's Chamber, Hordadef exclaimed that it would probably be our last visit to the grave.

"I thought you said this was not a grave," I asserted.

"I said no man was buried here. It was the grave of the god, Osiris."

"So the gods of Egypt were mortal?"

"No, only Osiris knew death. The rest are immortal and will be so until the end of time."

"Was Osiris a mortal and his body actually buried in here?"

"You are asking questions about things that concern only the gods and that only they can answer. Knowledge of such mysteries is not permitted man, Mr. Richard. All I can tell you is that this was his grave."

We took our seats on the floor and faced the north wall as we had the night before.

"The 2nd and 4th rows of the walls do not create images or symbols. Instead, their asymmetrically arranged points create a pattern that provides further insight into the Flood catastrophe."

He handed me two drawings that had only coordinates drawn on them (Figures #20 & 21). He then handed me another that had all eight of the coordinates, only they were marked with the names of stars and constellations (Figure #22). The plot showed that the points in the southern semicircle corresponded to a cluster of stars in the constellation of Sagittarius, while those in the northern semicircle corresponded to key stars in the constellations of Capricorn and Aquila.

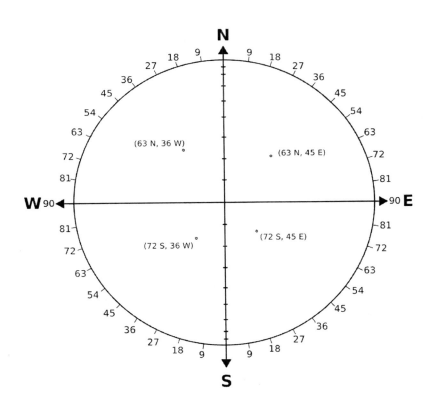

The 4th Celestial Sphere Coordinates

Figure 20

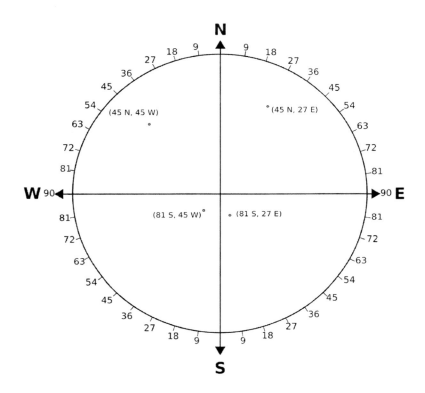

The 5th Celestial Sphere Coordinates

Figure 21

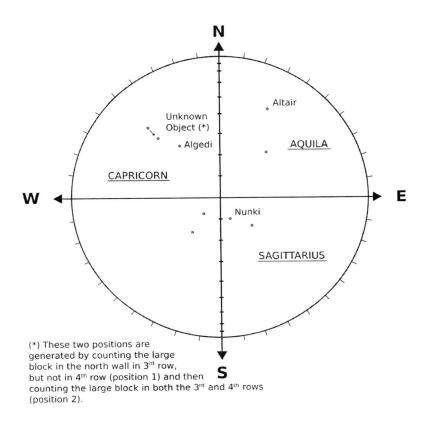

N

Unknown
Object (*)

. Altair

. Algedi

AQUILA

CAPRICORN

W ◄

► E

. Nunki

SAGITTARIUS

(*) These two positions are
generated by counting the large
block in the north wall in 3rd row,
but not in 4th row (position 1) and then
counting the large block in both the 3rd and 4th rows
(position 2).

S

Coordinates of 4th & 5th Spheres Combined
(Source of Earth's Destruction)
Figure 22

In the upper left quadrant of the plotting circle were two points in a line
with one another, one nearer the edge of the plotting circle and the other
closer to the center. As I read the caption beside the two points, the import
of the entire plot became apparent. It depicted the location in the heavens of
whatever it was that had destroyed the Earth!

"Horrific, is it not?" Hordadef said. "Now you see what the ancients saw
in the heavens that so terrified them. Now you can appreciate their fate as
they saw it."

"Yes." I was barely audible. "It must have been a truly terrifying prospect." I couldn't take my eyes off the drawing; it was a staggering sight and I was overwhelmed and deeply saddened by it. "I do have a question, though. Why didn't the architects of these symbols use the object's altitude and azimuth to directly plot its location, instead of creating this drawing?"

"Very good question. Very good, indeed, Mr. Richard! The reason is the heavens are constantly moving, so it was not possible to use altitude and azimuth coordinates to directly plot its location. Instead, the architects depicted a unique star pattern that would focus the viewer's attention on a particular area of the heavens, and then by plotting several nearby prominent stars for reference points they were able to depict the object's exact location."

"That makes sense."

We sat in silence for several long minutes before Hordadef resumed.

"Now we must use the language of myth to describe what actually happened. Myths are not always fairytales or children's stories, but oftentimes they are the only explanations possible for things that are beyond our ability to fully understand because they concern the affairs of God, the nature of sacred things, or because they are cosmic events on a scale of unimaginable proportions. Myths allow us to gain some limited understanding of these things, which by their very nature lie beyond us. Do you understand, Mr. Richard?"

"Yes."

"Very good, then. Let us proceed."

* * *

"We must first set the stage," Hordadef said, "by introducing the principal characters in the drama. This requires starting at the beginning of time and creation, according to the Egyptians. In this way we will learn not only who the characters are, but also their place in the cosmological order, which will give context to the epic events that surround the Flood. Are we agreed?"

"Yes."

"Very well. We begin with Ptah, who sits atop the Great Seat, the place beyond time, who conceived of the cosmos. He stirred the awareness of Atum Re, the creator god, who floated listlessly in the depths of the abyss. Atum Re awoke and found that he was tightly restrained within the surrounding coils of a great serpent, Apopis. After a tremendous struggle Atum Re broke free of Apopis's grip. He looked for something with which to raise himself out of the waters of the abyss and found the primordial support, or pillar. When Atum Re stood atop the pillar, that was the beginning of the cosmos.

"Next Atum Re called forth the names and destinies of all things that were or would be. First he named all the lesser gods, and the most ancient goddess, Neith, conceived of them. Atum Re then assigned them their positions in the heavens and fastened them to firm guide wires, that they might begin their endless flight about the Great Seat of Ptah. That was the beginning of time.

"Then Atum Re conceived of his children, Shu and Tefnut, and breathed life into them. Shu and Tefnut came forth as one and rose up from the abyss as a lotus. When the lotus reached the surface, its petals opened and Shu and Tefnut began. Thus light and order were born into the world. They in turn conceived and originated Geb and Nut, Earth and sky, who also emerged as one. Shu beheld the pair embracing one another and pulled Nut away from Geb, raising her high over his head and parting the waters of Earth and sky. Geb and Nut then conceived and brought forth five children: Osiris, Seth, Isis, Nephthys, and Horus the Elder, gods who walked the Earth. That was the beginning of Earth.

"Next Atum Re called forth man and the other mortal creatures. He fashioned mankind from his tears, assigned them their destinies, and breathed the breath of life into them. That was the beginning of mortal life on Earth.

"After Atum Re finished with creation, he appointed Osiris king to rule over all the Earth. Atum Re then rose up on high as the Sun and set sail across the heavens on the boat-of-millions-of-years. That was the beginning of earthly kingship.

"King Osiris ruled with firmness and justice, and there was peace and happiness throughout the world. He tamed the natures of men. Thus began civilization. But when Atum Re created mankind he placed in their souls both reason and choice: reason, that they might see and understand the nature of the cosmos and learn to live in harmony with it; and choice, that they might learn to follow reason, nurture their divine natures, and control their baser instincts. But he permitted them to do evil. That was the beginning of moral order in the world, and the struggle between good and evil.

"Osiris was king for many years. His brother Seth was jealous of him and began to incite men to conspire and raise their voices in anger against him. One night, on signal, Seth and his confederates rose in rebellion and attacked the palace of Osiris. The fighting was fierce, but Seth's forces swept Osiris's guards aside and entered the King's Chambers, where they found the king and drowned him. They celebrated their foul deed and raised Seth up to rule over them in place of Osiris. That was the beginning of chaos.

"Atum Re, who bore witness to these terrible events, cried out in anguish and anger over the death of his son. He sought the counsel of the other gods and bade the terrible goddess of death and suffering to punish mankind for their evil.

"The goddess took flight and tore across the heavens in a blind rage. As she neared Earth, she swung low in the heavens and aimed directly for it, her fury increasing with her approach. She found Seth and his companions and fixed them in her terrible gaze, descending upon them with unimaginable violence and destruction. Fire and Flood swept the Earth, and mankind suffered terribly and countless died. Thus did divine wrath deal with earthly evil. The terrible goddess would have slain all had not Atum Re heard their cries and taken pity on those few who survived. Atum Re bade her stay her hand and spare the remainder. Her rage abated and she returned to Heaven.

"These, Mr. Richard, are the myths that the Egyptians used to describe the events leading up to the Flood and why it happened. There is more to them, but we will leave that for another day. Now I will tell you what happened in real terms. But my words will not do justice to these events, as the language of myth is a far better vehicle.

"We will start with the words used by the Egyptian priest who spoke of these events in Plato's *Timaeus*:

> "There is a story, which even you have preserved [Solon], that once upon a time Phaeton, the son of Helios, having yoked the steeds in his father's chariot, because he was not able to drive them in the path of his father, burnt up all that was upon the Earth, and was himself destroyed by a thunderbolt. Now this has the form of a myth, but really signifies a declination of the bodies moving in the heavens around the Earth, and a great conflagration of things upon the Earth, which recurs after many long intervals…you remember a single deluge only, but there were many previous ones…before the greatest deluge of all…"

"The 'greatest deluge of all' was the Flood that is remembered in the stones of the Pyramid. And it was a body in the heavens, which either passed very close to the Earth or struck it, that caused the Flood.

"The people of the Earth saw the strange body in the heavens moving toward them and knew from long observation that it would either hit the Earth or come close enough to cause terrible destruction. They also knew they could do nothing to stop it from happening. So they prepared themselves for the impending catastrophe and arranged to preserve as much of their civilization and the knowledge that they had acquired as they could. This was the genesis for the Pyramid, which had been used as an observatory up until that time. Men continued to live their lives as the fated event bore down upon them. Many lived their lives in peace and tried to avoid all evil, but others mocked what was about to befall them and turned to lives of utter savagery and violence.

"As the body neared Earth, the ocean tides rose and fell to extreme levels and fierce storms caused tremendous destruction. People panicked, knowing the end was near, and sought shelter as best they could. Some moved into the mountains; others dug shelters in the ground, all to no avail. As the body drew closer, vast quantities of burning debris fell on the Earth, igniting great fires and adding to the terrible suffering of the people, who cried out pitifully for God's mercy. The winds howled and shrieked to maddening levels as the air was pushed before the approaching terror.

"In a blinding flash the object hit the Earth, which shuddered and shook violently. Those few men who had kept their wits about them watched in stunned disbelief as the stars appeared to fall from their places in the heavens. Earthquakes rent the ground, and volcanoes opened up and spewed fire and ash. Huge clouds of dust and smoke arose and joined with the clouds of innumerable storms that circled the Earth. Darkness descended everywhere, even where the Sun had shone earlier. Forests and buildings collapsed and caught fire. Destruction and death were everywhere, on an unimaginable scale.

"Then came an ear-shattering roar. The ground shook and trembled. Where flashes of lightning or flames of fire provided light, men beheld a vast wall of water, crushing and consuming everything as it rushed toward them. Those in its path screamed in terror, but no one heard. The few survivors who had fled to the high mountains and were still alive saw the water smash against the highlands and mountains to a great height, collapsing some of them. Then the water retreated, sucking everything behind it, seething and hissing as it drained away, back to the ocean, only to gather itself for another assault on the land.

"Again and again the great waves came until nothing was left but mud and rock. All else was destroyed and pulled into the ocean's bed or buried in deep muck. Snow and ice began covering vast stretches of land where it had never been seen. Chaos reigned. The Earth was destroyed. Where teeming life had once been there was nothing left, save Manetho's "Spirits of the Dead."

"Of the men God spared, most descended into madness and savagery, to forget and to survive. All memory of what had gone before and what had happened was lost to them and their descendants. Those who maintained their hold on reason struggled to comprehend what had happened and to nurture their faith that God would restore the world. These few remembered civilization and kept its blessings intact. But even they could not hold onto most of the memories of what had happened before the catastrophe. So it faded from them and passed into the realm of myth and legend."

Hordadef closed his eyes and lowered his head. He remained so for several minutes.

When he opened his eyes, he raised his head, turned to me, and said it was time to go. We stood up together and departed the Chamber in silence. We exited the Pyramid several minutes later and returned to the parked cab. Then we drove off and returned to the hotel, where Hordadef pulled the cab over to the side and I opened the door to get out. I turned to ask him what time we would next meet. He said ten o'clock in the morning and we both said our farewells for the evening.

It had been a very long and momentous day for me.

9

Birth of Horus and Resurrection of the Earth

I awoke before sunrise and lay in bed for quite some time, thinking not only about the previous day's momentous events, but also about everything I had learned so far. The legends of the Arabs and Jews were apparently all true! The Pyramid had been built to memorialize the Flood, and Hordadef had shown me the star charts, terrestrial globes, and celestial spheres in it, just as the legends claimed. Apparently the common source for all the legends was the Pyramid itself and the ancient Egyptians.

I was thrilled, but none of the information I'd acquired was due to my own efforts. It was all Hordadef's. I was humbled by his staggering knowledge of the Pyramid . . . and by its anonymous designers and builders, who were not only men of great knowledge and technical expertise, but deeply religious men as well. I felt honored that Hordadef had taught me and I hardly knew how to thank him.

I had come to Egypt hardly expecting to find anything and fully prepared to end my academic project. I suspected that the Pyramid was something more than just a grandiose tomb for the glorification of one Pharaoh. But I had nothing to base my suspicions on, other than that the tomb theory seemed a little too far-fetched, given the immense size of the Pyramid and the unimaginable technical expertise that had gone into its construction. The legends spun by the Arabs and Jews of the Middle Ages seemed like a reasonable alternate theory, though I had to admit that some aspects of these legends also appeared a little far-fetched. But Hordadef's lessons were convincing and provided proof of their veracity.

It was strange. I had certainly hoped to find some limited evidence supporting the validity of the legends, enough perhaps to enable me to complete my thesis. I hardly expected to learn that the Pyramid might belong to a far more ancient age. The Flood story, too, had seemed to me nothing more than a simple tale from the Bible. Hardly an event to be taken seriously, much less one that had actually occurred. Yet, these things were apparently all true, forcing a dramatic reassessment and realignment in my understanding of several things.

The Pyramid's accepted chronological moorings in Egypt's Old Kingdom were slipping. It was drifting back into the murky, uncharted waters of an uncertain time, far beyond my knowledge or understanding, or anyone else's for that matter. The Flood story, on the other hand, was emerging from the shadows of that same distant age. What did all this mean?

There was far too much for me to fully contemplate for the moment, much less comprehend. The mere thought was thrilling and extremely unsettling at the same time. I realized I might not be the only one to feel the weight of this knowledge or the challenges it presented, nor the only one unnerved by it. I suspected that all of this would reverberate for a long time to come, and have unforeseen ramifications.

All because of the stories of a modest and unassuming Egyptian cab driver! Everything came back to Hordadef. Who was he? How did he (and perhaps no one else) know these things? That was the greatest mystery of all.

It had escaped my notice that the Sun had risen while I dallied with my thoughts. I looked at my watch. It was almost nine. Time to get up and get on with the day.

Hordadef was waiting for me by the time I exited the hotel courtyard. We were soon walking among the same *mastabas* we had passed the day before.

"Are we going back to the Sphinx?" I asked.

"No, to a spot short of it."

We reached a bluff and left the path to sit among some unremarkable ruins from a New Kingdom Temple that was largely destroyed, but it provided a spectacular vantage point for viewing the Sphinx. If Hordadef had brought me here expecting privacy, he had made a mistake. Many others were taking advantage of the location to take pictures of the Sphinx and the other ruins below the bluff. He seemed unfazed by their presence and was soon engrossed in the day's lesson.

"Now, Mr. Richard, we left off yesterday with the Earth having been destroyed by a celestial body entering the solar system. The terrible initial shocks of the catastrophe lingered for some time, but soon tapered off. The seas calmed and returned to their beds. The storms and earthquakes became less frequent and less intense.

"For the few who survived and were aware of what had happened, everything was changed. The Earth turned in uncustomary fashion, without regularity or consistency, and its orientation to the heavens had altered utterly. The North celestial pole pointed to a location far removed from Vega in the Lyre. It would focus on one location and then suddenly move off toward another without warning.

"The weather also changed. Egypt was no longer a desert. Rains came with great frequency and soon turned the desert lands into grasslands, and eventually forests began to appear. Elsewhere in the world, similar dramatic changes occurred. Vast stretches of Europe were covered in ice and snow, and the ocean beyond was a much shrunken remnant of what it had been. Its level lay hundreds of feet below where it once was, and its steep banks were covered in mud and rocks. Great mounds of debris that had been pulled down from the lands above by the waves of the Flood lay everywhere along its banks and in its shallows. Interminable fogs frequently covered the area, and nowhere did one hear the voice of life. The only sounds that one heard were the terrifying roars and grinding sounds from the many earthquakes that continued to tear the ruined land. And most of the few, pitiful survivors of mankind had reverted to lives of utter savagery and lived as animals. .

"I told you that the Descending Passage of the Pyramid was aimed at Vega, which was very near the North celestial pole at the time of the catastrophe, and that the great age at the time was just entering Cancer. This, as I've stated, is illogical because the North celestial pole should have been in a far different location in the heavens at the onset of the Age of Cancer, based on our present understanding of astronomical history. So either the ancient astronomers made a gross error or something happened to cause the celestial pole to move from its expected location. And indeed something did happen to it. The celestial body that struck the Earth caused the Earth to roll over. To fall off its axis, so to speak.

"In technical terms what happened is that the orientation of the Earth's axis of rotation, which behaves like a huge rotating gyroscope, underwent a sudden and extreme motion from the tremendous force of the impact. Since the Earth's axis is not fixed, the power of the impact combined with the Earth's turning motion forced the axis of rotation down and away from the point of impact. Then the Earth's rotation carried this downward motion considerably to the left of where it had been along the customary path of the North celestial pole. In other words, the pole itself moved across the heavens.

"A gyroscope with a fixed axis generally responds to an external blow by moving down and away from the direction of the blow and then twisting around, along the direction of its rotation, some 90° or more until the force of the blow has been absorbed. Then its axis of rotation returns it to its previous upright position. A gyroscope whose axis is not fixed behaves similarly, but its movements in response to an external force are much more radical.

"As I said, this is the technical explanation for what happened. The practical effect was that the Earth's axis was forced down and turned until the North celestial pole came to rest temporarily near Orion and Sirius. How long it stayed in this location is anyone's guess. Besides, the question is illogical since time as previously defined no longer had meaning. And therein lay the greatest effect of the catastrophe: the death of Divine Order."

"I don't mean to interrupt," I said, "but how do you know all of this? It's just astounding to me that you would know all of this."

"This what?"

"These things about gyroscopes and their motions."

"Look Mr. Richard, just because I am entrusted with knowledge from my ancestors doesn't mean that I can't update or add to it, does it?"

"No, of course not."

"Well, then. Hordadef has been faithful to the trust placed in him by his ancestors. But he has neither been complacent nor neglectful of his responsibilities, and he has studiously sought ways to keep current the knowledge entrusted to him. Would you not agree that this is important?"

"Of course, it only makes sense."

"Well, then. Since there is no disagreement on this point, I will continue. I told you early in our relationship that time is motion and motion is time. This is not a trivial thing, Mr. Richard, for without the regular and predictable motion of the Earth, time has no meaning whatsoever. Clock time or mechanical time is predicated on solar time, which is based on the rotation of the Earth. And if solar time has no meaning, then clock time becomes an arbitrary and meaningless frame of reference. And if the Earth has lost its alignment with the heavens, orientation and direction also have no meaning.

"We take the blessings of order for granted, so much so that we assume they are our birthright. That is a mistake, for without order there is chaos. 'I will get up tomorrow at seven o'clock and go to work at my office, which is five miles north of where I live' becomes an absurd statement in the absence of order. What if the Sun were to rise tomorrow from a point far to the northeast and then set far to the northwest after 9 hours, and the day after arise from a location even farther north and then set in the direction that it set the day before, but after only 8 hours? What if that first day lasted a total of 23 hours of mechanical time, but the second lasted for only 22 hours? Would seven o'clock in the morning mean the same thing on both days? Would north have any meaning without the orderly and predictable motions of the Sun and the heavens to provide cardinality and orientation? Of course not, and that is why order is so fundamental to our existence. Without it, there is no frame of reference to center our lives around and civilization becomes impossible. Reason is cut off from the order that gave rise to it and from which it originated, and so withers and dies.

"Order is truly the gift of Heaven. That is why the ancient Egyptian priests concluded every religious service or celebration by raising the figure of *Mayet*, or Divine Order, up to the assembled people so that all could see and give thanks to God for it. No longer do we give thanks to God for this great blessing, but there was a time when people pleaded with God to restore it and cried out from the endless misery they suffered from its loss.

"The Flood was a terrible catastrophe, but the loss of order threatened humanity's continued existence. It suggested to people that further devastation from the heavens might befall them at any moment. All of this challenged their reason, their divine link with God Himself, for without reason there can only be madness and death. That is the very definition of chaos, and its name was Seth—the god of violence, he who tore free of his mother's womb and unleashed unimaginable misery and suffering on the world. He who rebelled against God and slew Osiris, the king.

"In ancient Egypt, Osiris became the universal god of resurrection, but in his original form he was quite literally the axis of the Earth. This is why his sacred symbol, the *djed* column, has four rings around it that correspond to the four great rings of the Earth: the two tropics and the two polar circles. The two tropics define the limits of the Sun's apparent movements, while the two polar circles define the orientation of the Earth with respect to Ptah, the North pole of the ecliptic. They are also the manifestation of order on Earth and its link to Heaven, and the source of all time and measure. This order permits life to exist and gives rise to civilization. Without it, both are threatened and cannot long survive.

"After Seth slew Osiris, Isis and Nephthys recovered his body and hid it in the Earth, where they watched over it lest Seth find it and tear it to pieces. There they prayed for Osiris's recovery, begging him to 'rise up on one side.' In response to their prayers, God restored Osiris to life, but he remained listless and unresponsive, much like the axis of the Earth after the Flood. Isis managed to become pregnant by him and eventually she bore a son, whom she named Horus. She raised Horus in secret lest Seth, who sat on Osiris's throne, would find him and do him harm. Horus grew to manhood under the watchful eyes of Isis and Nephthys.

"Once he came of age, Horus set out to avenge his father's death and claim his throne for himself. The fight between Seth and Horus was long and violent, but Horus was triumphant and the heavenly company of gods confirmed the throne of Osiris to him. Horus descended to his father's grave to tell him the great news. At this point in religious ceremonies in ancient Egypt the sacred *djed* column was raised. Horus became a falcon and flew off to the ramparts of the heavens, and order was restored to Earth.

"I have used the language of myth to describe actual events that transpired on Earth and in the heavens, too. The axis of the Earth, which had fallen and pointed to an unaccustomed location in the heavens, began to right itself, just as a gyroscope would. But the recovery was accompanied by the great violence of earthquakes and volcanoes. This great struggle was played out in the heavens. The axis of rotation began its recovery in fits and starts before moving decisively back to the great ring that surrounds Ptah, the path slowly traced out by the North celestial pole as it rotates around Ptah. The principal locus of the Earth's struggle to right itself appeared to be Ursa Major, or the Great Bear, which is why ancient Egyptians identified that constellation with Seth. It was there that the great fight between Seth and Horus appeared to play itself out to observers on Earth.

"As a falcon, Horus now circles the Great Seat as the North celestial pole. As the current North celestial pole, Horus has been given his rightful place in the heavens, the seat formerly occupied by his father. Osiris was restored to life, but Atum Re decreed that he would remain in the Earth until the end of time, as his former seat in the heavens has now been assigned to his son Horus. Thus Earth was restored and order returned under the reign of Horus. Osiris, who was in the Earth, became its axis—raised up from the dead, 'raised up on one side'—and restored to Earth its previous slanted aspect.

"One final item needs addressing on this topic. How did the Earth recover? This is not an easy question to answer because it is rooted in the how and why the Earth began its motions in the first place. Ultimately, this is a matter known only by God, but we may at least discuss it to the extent that we can. As in the foregoing parts of our discussion, I will present my argument in both practical and mythological terms.

"In mythological terms the Earth was resurrected from death and reincarnated by the god Sokar, whose role is to preserve the primordial memory of God's original purpose in creation. It is he who awakens the souls of the deceased and returns them to life, much as he rekindles the fires of the Sun each night before it begins its ascent the following day. Sokar remembers the things God originally proclaimed. He remembers the divine purpose of every motion in the heavens and on Earth.

"There may in fact be a part of the Earth that retains the memory of its original motions, which allows it to sustain its movements over time and to recover from external forces that upset these movements. At its core the Earth is believed to be solid, because of the compressive forces of the great mass around it. So even though the heat from this burden may be great enough to cause the center to liquefy, the mass above it is great enough to overcome the force of heat and keep it in solid form. But above this solid core, the heat is strong enough to keep everything in liquid form. If this is so, when the Earth was struck by the celestial body that precipitated the Flood catastrophe, the upper areas of the Earth above the core rolled over and it shifted its axis of rotation in response to the force of the impact. But the solid core was not affected by it and remained in its customary attitude and moved in its accustomed motions. It was the motions of the core that literally preserved the memory of the motions of the Earth and, after the catastrophe, returned the Earth to its previous attitude and motions.

"Interestingly, Sokar is always depicted as inhabiting the center of Earth, the heart of the underworld. Perhaps there are direct parallels between him and Earth's core, and their intended purposes are identical. Both are memory or spirit. Since Sokar is God's memory, he is honored—as are Ptah and Osiris—with the epithet Lord of Eternity.

"In any case, the Earth did recover and was returned to its previous orientation and movements. But, as I mentioned, the location of its celestial pole had changed dramatically. Because the Earth was able to recover its rotational velocity relatively quickly after the impact, when the Earth's axis returned to its upright position the Earth was able to resume its previous location and progress along the band of the zodiac with little or no change. This is why the North celestial pole could shift so radically without a noticeable change to the great calendar. And this is why people cannot understand how the North celestial pole could have resided near Vega, while the Earth was nearing the Age of Cancer, when the catastrophe struck. It was because the pole had shifted dramatically while the time of the Great Age remained roughly the same. When the Earth recovered its former upright orientation, the great age was leaving Leo and entering Cancer, just where it had been before the Flood catastrophe."

His pause allowed me time to notice the many people constantly passing by, up and down the path, stopping to view the Sphinx. I was curious why Hordadef had picked such a public and highly traveled area for this story. I looked down on the Sphinx and the other nearby ruins. No question that this was a magnificent vantage point for viewing them. I was admiring the view when Hordadef spoke again.

"That, Mr. Richard, is the story of how the Earth rolled over after being struck by the aberrant celestial body, which almost destroyed all life, and how it recovered from that catastrophe. As you've heard, much of this is spoken of in the sacred myths of the ancient Egyptians. These seemingly simple tales recall the most horrific event ever to befall the human race, and how God spared us from total annihilation and restored the Earth to its former circumstances.

"Do you know why I brought you to this spot?"

"Because of the view?" I ventured.

"Yes, in part, but there is a larger purpose. This spot was formerly occupied by a structure built in the era of ancient Egypt's New Kingdom. Presumably it was a temple, though that is largely immaterial. It is gone now, but its focus was the Sphinx, which people in those days had come to revere as a god. Think of that, Mr. Richard. Here is the Sphinx, the "father of terrors," carved as a reminder of the Flood, yet the descendants of those who carved the Sphinx and survived the Flood came to admire and possibly even worship it. How is such a thing possible?"

Before I could respond, he answered his own question.

"Because people forget, or they allow important things to grow trivial in their minds as they go about their lives. Such are the vagaries of the human temperament. Knowledge fades, beliefs grow weak, and gradually people lose the memory of that which they should never forget. What their forebears swore to remember forever is replaced with a simplistic wonder and enchantment with the relics and events of the past without any true understanding of what they originally meant. Then it becomes possible to erect a structure like the one that used to occupy this site. People come to it for the view and the excitement of being among strange and exotic structures. And because they are so disconnected from the past, it is even possible for them to cast objects such as the Sphinx in a light never intended by their authors and to stoop to worshiping them. Can you imagine?"

"Sadly, yes. Knowing people, I can easily imagine it," I said.

He turned to look out at the Sphinx, the resignation in his voice evident. "Nothing endures forever. Nothing. Perhaps that is the way of man and nothing ever can or will change it." He stood. "Come, Mr. Richard. I want to show you one other place today and it will take awhile for us to drive there."

I stood, too. As we started down the path between the *mastabas*, I thought about his earlier lesson and it brought a question to mind. "I don't quite understand how the Pyramid is tied into the concept of Divine Order."

"Excuse me? Excuse me, Mr. Richard? Have you not been paying attention at all to what I have been saying these past many days? Everything about the Pyramid speaks to order: its location, its orientation, its measures of distance, the knowledge embodied in its stones, its relationship to the heavens and the movements of the Sun and stars, its measures of time. All these things are order, Mr. Richard. How is it that this is lost on you? Do you really not understand?"

"No, I just didn't quite appreciate the connection."

"Mr. Richard, the Pyramid is all about order. The order that exists between Heaven and Earth. All of the many things that I have shown you and told you, with the exception of the Flood catastrophe, have been about this order. As I said at the very beginning of our contract, Earth, Heaven, and Pyramid are the same. What relates them to one another is Divine Order. Do we understand this?"

"Yes. It's not always easy to grasp these things in their entirety, though accepting them individually has not been too difficult."

"Mr. Richard, I think you, like most modern men, have accepted the blessings of Divine Order for so long without question that you take them for granted. So much so that you cannot imagine life without them. That is one of the most fundamental errors someone can make. These things do not belong to humankind by inherent right. They are truly the gift of God. Unless you see this, you will not fully understand and appreciate all that I am teaching you."

"I guess it's proving more difficult than I thought."

"Maybe so, Mr. Richard. But you must remind yourself of this every day. Perhaps we should conclude for today. I was going to take you to Heliopolis, but I don't think the trip will be particularly productive. The city of Cairo has covered up much of the ancient site, which makes it hard to imagine what was there and how important it was to Egypt and the world. It might be better to talk about it during our trip tomorrow instead."

"Our trip?"

"Yes, we need to go to Dashur and Saqqara to see the pyramids there. They are relevant to our lessons. I think you will learn a lot tomorrow, Mr. Richard. Yes, tomorrow you will learn a lot more about the sacred things of Egypt."

"I look forward to it," I said as we neared the hotel. "What time should we meet?"

"Let's say tomorrow morning at half past seven. It will be a long trip and a tiring one because most of it is in the desert. So we'll need to get an early start."

"Okay then, half past seven it is." We shook hands. When he turned and started toward his cab, I called after him. "Hordadef! I just want to say how much I appreciate everything you've taught me. I'll try harder to fully understand it all."

"No, no, Mr. Richard. You are doing fine. Besides, our contract specifies that everything must be to your full satisfaction. Otherwise there is no charge. That is what truly concerns me, Mr. Richard. If you do not understand, then how can you be satisfied? And if you are not satisfied, then how can I be paid for my services? That is a most serious problem for me, as I'm sure you can appreciate. I cannot work for nothing. So we will see you in the morning then."

He entered his cab and drove off. I waved and he honked his horn in acknowledgement. I spent the rest of the day reviewing the notes I had taken, trying to make sense of everything. It was an almost overwhelming chore.

10

Priests and Pyramids

The morning was quite cool, so we kept the windows rolled up as Hordadef headed out of town. Once we'd turned off the main road into Cairo and headed south, there was considerably less traffic and we picked up speed. Hordadef asked if I had any questions about any of my lessons and I said I didn't for the moment. He looked at me as if he wanted to say something, then turned his attention back to the road. Finally he asked whether I'd heard of Heliopolis.

"Yes," I answered.

"Good! Can you tell me when the city was founded and by whom?"

"No, I can't. I don't believe anyone knows that...except maybe you."

He laughed and thanked me for my confidence in him. "Heliopolis, which is Greek for City of the Sun, was known as Innu, Egyptian for City of the Pillar. It was founded not long after the Flood by those few priests who had survived the catastrophe. The city was located close to the Nile, just above the beginning of the vast delta region, so it had fairly easy access to both the river and the sea that lay beyond. Originally it was located in fairly lush surroundings, but when Egypt began to dry out again, the city found itself in the desert.

"From the very beginning Heliopolis was renowned far and wide for the great knowledge and understanding of its priests. They held themselves apart from the rest of humanity that had survived the Flood out of fear of them, as most were dangerous and unpredictable. For their part, these scattered, savage remnants of mankind respected and feared the priests for their knowledge and strange ways. They referred to the priests as watchers or *watcher angels* because of their strange habit of watching the heavens incessantly. Their insignia was the five-pointed star, which they held to be the pattern for all order and harmony in the universe.

"When the catastrophe was long forgotten by the rest of humanity, the priests of Heliopolis remembered it and would never forget. They preserved much of the knowledge and culture of Egypt from the devastation of the Flood: religion, writing, mathematics, geometry, astronomy, medicine, architecture, agriculture, animal husbandry, and many arts and crafts. All were preserved. But primarily they preserved the ancient order in the form of time and distance measures, as well as maintaining water clocks, calendars, and measuring devices. As humanity's numbers began to recover from the catastrophe, the priests gradually befriended and taught some of them their accumulated knowledge. Civilization slowly began to reappear.

"The priests were aware that learned people in other locations had also survived the Flood. As the ability to travel to distant lands, especially by ship, slowly increased, they made contact with them. They traveled to those lands and received visitors from them, too. All travel was by ship, which gave the priests knowledge of navigation and sailing. In fact, priests and mariners depended on each other. Priests relied on mariners for their skills in handling ships and sailing, while mariners relied on priests for celestial navigation and charting. They were partners in the quest to understand what had happened to the Earth: how much damage it had suffered and whether it was permanent. This quest spanned ages and occupied learned men around the world.

"In the meantime, as the population continued to recover, the priests knew that one day their numbers would reach a point that required centralized government and formal societal organization to establish civil order. This would be a mixed blessing. People would have access to the vast resources only a government could command, but tyranny and violence were possible on a comparable scale. In this land the moment arrived some 5,000 years ago with the King or Pharaoh named Menes, the first to rule all of Egypt.

"The priests had been on good terms with their fellow Egyptians for many years, and they welcomed the new rulers, offering praise for their accomplishments. The priests helped Menes and his court establish the organization of government and then offered to help them run it, providing scribes and other priests with specialized knowledge and expertise. This symbiotic relationship existed from the beginning, and it persisted throughout the thousands of years that Egyptian civilization endured.

"Indeed their example would be followed elsewhere in the world by newly emerging societies and cultures. Heliopolis became the most renowned center of learning in the ancient world, its priests the wisest of men. Heliopolis survived until its priests and their vast collection of records were taken to Alexandria to the great library established by Alexander the Great. A few older priests clung to their ancient ways in the ruins of their once great temples, but eventually all succumbed and Heliopolis was abandoned and the silence of the desert reclaimed it. A place of light for thousands of years, it had preserved civilization until humanity was again ready to receive its blessings.

"One of the first requests the priests made of their new patrons was assistance in digging out and restoring a number of important structures that had been ravaged by the Flood. Among these were the structures on the Giza plateau, including the Pyramid. Egyptian citizens had long been aware of the great structures on Giza and were amazed by them, but feared them, too. These unimaginably large and awesome structures could only be the works of gods, so they avoided them lest the gods take offense at their trespass and punish them. The structures were referred to as the *thrones of the gods*.

"After Menes unified Egypt, one of his first official acts, as urged and planned by the priests, was to turn the Nile away from the area around Saqqara and Giza and resurrect a great city destroyed by the Flood. The new city would be called White Walls, or *Ankh-Tawy*, or the Residence City. Later the Greeks named it Memphis. It remained a large and prominent city throughout Egypt's long history, until the rise of Cairo. Today it has virtually disappeared, its remains swallowed up again by the river."

"So Memphis existed before the Flood?" I asked.

"Yes, but of its history before the Flood virtually nothing is known."

"Why did the priests feel it was so important to resurrect it? Surely it would have made more sense to simply build it again in an area not subject to flooding."

"You're right, but the priests no doubt recalled the importance of the city in former days and felt it should be refounded on its historic site. The area had once been protected by a system of levees, and a great dam fifteen miles upstream had diverted the river around it. Maybe the task before Menes was simply to repair the dam, as the protective walls were largely, if not completely, intact. After that the city could simply be dried out by allowing the accumulated water in it to evaporate. The only remaining task would be to remove the accumulated silt."

"Sounds plausible. But what about the Pyramid. Did it suffer damage as well?"

"We will take that issue up later, if it's all right with you."

"Of course. You're the teacher."

"Very good! We're almost at Dashur. We'll turn up ahead and then drive into the desert for a short distance to the two large stone pyramids there: the Bent Pyramid and the Red Pyramid. Both supposedly were built by Pharaoh

Sneferu, the father of Khufu, whose name will forever be linked with the Great Pyramid."

* * *

At some distance away the tops of the two pyramids loomed over the palm trees along the floodplain. They looked the same size for some time, even after we turned off the main road. When we cleared the fertile areas and climbed into the desert, they still looked to be similar in size. But as we approached the Red Pyramid, its size increased exponentially. It was impressive, but not nearly as impressive as the Great Pyramid. Its considerably smaller slope made it somewhat squatter, less dramatic in appearance.

Hordadef parked his cab among a few other cars and we strode toward the pyramid. I saw several people walking around it taking pictures, and the contrast only added to my impression of its massiveness. About a mile to the south stood the Bent Pyramid, which still appeared to be the same size as when I had first seen it from the car. But I knew that in fact it was almost the same size as the Red Pyramid.

We walked along the pyramid's north face to its eastern corner until Hordadef said to stop. Directly south of where we stood we could see the Bent Pyramid. We found a low stone structure that appeared to have been the base of a wall and sat on it.

"Mr. Richard," Hordadef began, "these two pyramids were called the Shining Pyramids. They and another one farther south at Meidum, which was also supposedly built by Pharaoh Sneferu, were used by the Heliopolitan priests to study the Sun and the heavens to determine if the Flood had caused any lasting changes to Earth's orientation and movements. Two and quite possibly all three of these structures existed before the Flood, but not in the form you see them today. All were heavily damaged by the catastrophe. After the Pharaohs came to power in Egypt, these pyramids were first repaired and then considerably modified at the direction of the priests.

"Several important pieces of knowledge had been lost or rendered obscure by the long intervening years between the Flood and the rebirth of civilization: the knowledge that the Earth rotated on its axis and that it orbited the Sun. Many priests reverted to the understandable but erroneous belief that the Sun orbited the Earth. After all, this is what their eyes told them when they observed the Sun's motions. And the thought that the Earth revolved around the Sun was almost impossible to conceive.

"Two astronomical issues particularly concerned the priests and they could not resolve them without the help of the government: one, whether the catastrophe had altered the motions of the Sun; and two, the nature and degree of change to the Earth's orientation with respect to Ptah. From these concerns a number of questions arose. Did the Sun still move along its accustomed path around the Earth? Was the North celestial pole still 24° from Ptah and rotating about it as before? And if the answers to these two questions was yes, then what was the rate of these movements? Finding the answers to these questions involved regular and detailed observations of the heavens over many, many years. It was an intergenerational project. But the priests were accustomed to long-term work and had both the patience and tenacity to see such projects through. After all, they had survived the Flood and endured the many years since.

"Along with reclaiming Memphis, the priests made repairing these pyramids a high priority so that they could use them to observe the North celestial pole and the Sun. But not long after they had been repaired and returned to use as observatories, a bright young priest named Imhotep came up with a startling theory: the apparent whirling motion of the stars as they circled the North celestial pole wasn't dependent on the motion of the stars, but on the rotation of the Earth about its axis (Figure #23). This theory probably wouldn't have provoked the reaction that it did if Imhotep had not been so close to the royal family. He and Pharaoh Zoser, the then-reigning king, had studied together at Heliopolis and remained close personal friends. Over the years of their long relationship, Zoser appointed Imhotep to a number of prominent and powerful positions in the royal court. As a result, when he spoke his fellow priests had to give him great deference. His theory, discomforting as it was to the established beliefs of the other priests, had to be taken seriously.

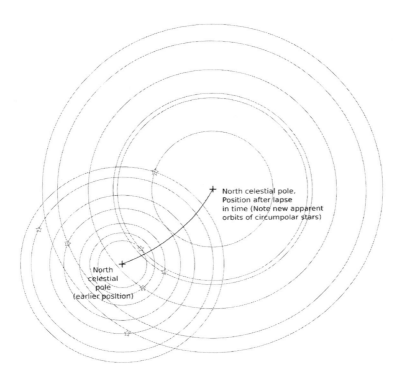

The Movement of the Whorl Around
the North Celestial Pole as it Circles Ptah
Figure 23

"When asked if any other observable phenomenon supported such a radical theory, he stated that if indeed the Earth was a rotating sphere, the observed apparent velocity of the Sun would vary with latitude, appearing to become progressively slower across the same measure latitudinal distance as an observer moved from the equator toward the poles. The reason for this, he explained, was inherent in the characteristics of a rotating sphere: a point on its midpoint would have to move considerably faster than a point located near the ends of the sphere to travel the same measured distance. In terrestrial terms, a point on the equator has a greater distance to travel to complete a circuit about the Earth within 24 hours than does a point nearer to one of the poles. In other words, the Sun's apparent velocity appears to vary with latitude. And if it does, while the measured distance observed remains the same, the apparent transit time of the Sun across the measured distance has to vary with latitude, too.

"When asked if he could prove his theory, he proposed a suitable test. The movement of the Sun's shadows thrown by the Dashur pyramid—the Bent Pyramid—across a shadow wall of known dimensions, located north of and parallel to the northern face of the pyramid, could be timed and then compared with similar observations at the pyramid at Meidum. The priests agreed, since the test was relatively simply to conduct, and set about making the necessary preparations. The tests were performed again and again, from approximately ten o'clock in the morning to two in the afternoon each day from October through March. In every case the times needed for the shadows to move a certain distance across the northern shadow walls of the two pyramids varied, with the times at Dashur being longer than those at Meidum.

"While many of the priests were extremely disconcerted, they were unwilling to concede the point just yet. They convinced Pharaoh that possible discrepancies between the clocks at the two widely separated locations could account for the observed differences. To eliminate such error they proposed building a second pyramid at Dashur just north and slightly west of the existing one, then timing the observations with the same clock to preclude the possibility of clock error.

"This significant undertaking would take years. Calculations indicated that the pyramid needed to be at least 105 meters high to serve its intended function. Priests would measure the transit time of the Sun across a specific distance on the north and south faces of the pyramid as it gradually moved between the Tropic of Capricorn and the equator with the seasons. But this time the tests would run from nine o'clock in the morning to three in the afternoon each day, October through March. The existing pyramid was a little taller than required, so it needed to be lowered to 105 meters also. This was accomplished by removing its top and rebuilding it so that its height and slope exactly matched those of the new pyramid.

"The priests pointed out that since the existing pyramid was being used to monitor the movements of the North celestial pole at night, further accommodations would have to be made so that this function could continue. After considerable study it was agreed that a smaller pyramid could be built south of the existing one. If a fire pit and wall were built between it and the existing pyramid, the fire would reflect off the smaller pyramid and illuminate the tip of the larger one against the night sky so that the location and movements of the North celestial pole could be closely observed.

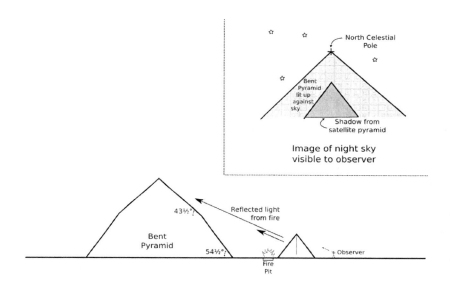

Measuring the Movements of the North Celestial Pole

Figure 24

The illumination would serve this purpose without being so intense as to interfere with the observations. More importantly, these changes would not interfere with the additional plans to use the pyramid to measure the Sun's motions.

"By the time the new pyramid was built and the existing one modified, however, both Imhotep and Pharaoh Zoser were long dead, and several succeeding Pharaohs had come and gone, as well. Progress on the two projects at Dashur proceeded apace, though slowly, until the ascension of Pharaoh

Sneferu to the throne. Under his reign they received the government's full attention and the necessary resources, which allowed both to be completed before his death.

"The Dashur projects had taken on even more significance, as Imhotep had further refined his theory before his death. Not only did the Earth rotate on its axis, as he had proposed earlier, but since the axis was permanently slanted some 24°, the Earth also had to revolve around the Sun or the seasons would never change. This further elaboration was not greeted with enthusiasm and the priests looked forward to disproving both of Imhotep's theories once the two pyramids were completed."

I had to interrupt. "How did the Heliopolitan priests know so much about the heavens and yet they didn't know that the Earth rotated on its axis and orbited the Sun?"

"They did, or rather they had," Hordadef replied. "But this knowledge was lost or discredited over the years between the catastrophe and the return of civilization to Earth. Also, those records that had managed to survive the Flood were based on a relative position plot with the Earth at the center, as it was the simplest and most effective means of transmitting this information. They probably believed that this was more important than using charts with the Sun at the center, and that anyone smart enough to interpret the relative position plot most likely knew that the solar system operated differently than that. In any case, the priests' inability to perform detailed observations of the heavens for several thousand years following the Flood probably allowed error to creep into the knowledge transmitted between the many generations of priests who followed."

I had another question. "How do you know all of these things about Imhotep and no one else does?"

"My father told me."

I recalled a similar response from him from our earlier conversations. I wanted to pursue the issue, but I knew it was probably futile to do so. Instead I said, "And I suppose he heard it from his father and so on and so on."

"How did you know?"

"I figured that was the case."

"Well, at least you're learning something." He laughed. "Come, let's drive down to the other pyramid. It is well worth seeing and its singular shape has inspired man's curiosity for ages."

We retraced our steps across the front of the Red Pyramid. As we made our way to the car, Hordadef said that the low wall we'd been sitting on ran around the whole perimeter of the pyramid and had also been used to measure the movements of the Sun to tell time. However, the priests felt that tracking the Sun by the movement of its shadow was not precise enough to prove Imhotep's theories.

The ride to the Bent Pyramid only took a couple of minutes. It was far more impressive than its northern counterpart. The angle of the base was much steeper, and the angle of the upper portion made a distinct break. Much of its original outer casing was still in place, which gave it a smoother, more finished look. There was something captivating about its incongruous appearance.

We walked along the pyramid's western side, where Hordadef pointed out the remains of its shadow wall, which completely surrounded the pyramid. I asked how the priests were able to communicate between the two pyramids and time the movements of the Sun's shadows at each, using only one clock.

"Very good question," he said. "They used fixed mirrors that automatically signaled the exact instant when the Sun reached its starting and stopping points."

"Makes sense," I said. "So the priests at the northern Shining Pyramid signaled their colleagues at the southern pyramid to mark the measurement's starting and stopping points at their pyramid on the same clock used at the southern Shining Pyramid for this purpose. In this way observations made at both pyramids were timed with the same clock, which precluded any possibility of clock error."

"Very good! That's exactly right! When observations commenced at the Shining Pyramids, it was readily apparent that the results of the previous tests at Dashur and Meidum had not been wrong. However, as I said earlier the shadow walls were not used for this purpose. Instead, the time that it took for the Sun's light to disappear from each pyramid's eastern face to the time that its light appeared on the western face were measured and compared. In each and every instance that this test was run, the time observed at the Red Pyramid was 3 seconds longer than at the Bent Pyramid. The light on the pyramids' eastern and western faces, along their 43.5° slopes, appeared or disappeared in a flash, so there was no mistaking the precise start and stop times for the observations. And as the fixed mirrors automatically signaled these measurements, there was no room for human error. The measurements were precise and accurate.

"Imhotep was proved right again! It was the Earth that rotated on its axis about the Sun and not the Sun about the Earth. With Imhotep dead, however, the priests who opposed his theory refused to concede the point. They convinced Pharaoh Sneferu to conduct similar tests at Meidum, which would entail modifying the existing pyramid and building a second one, thus creating a matched pair like the ones at Dashur. Sneferu approved the proposal and sent workers to begin the project. By the time Sneferu died significant progress had been made on modifying the existing pyramid, but work was immediately suspended until the new Pharaoh, Khufu, could review the project. It was risky to assume that he would continue it. The effort and expense involved were enormous, so official sanction was critical.

"Khufu, on the advice of his closest counselors, ruled that there was no reason to continue the Meidum pyramid projects because the results of the tests at Dashur were conclusive. Imhotep's theories were correct and should be acknowledged by all. All work at Meidum was permanently stopped. Today the pyramid looks much the same as it did 4,500 years ago, partially modified but unfinished.

"Imhotep's theories were accepted by a number of the priests, but only begrudgingly acknowledged by most. Few priests could comprehend and explain it. For many, many years it remained a smoldering controversy in their ranks, which quickly lead to the formation of bitterly opposed factions. The Shining Pyramids were abandoned not long after, and with the passing of time even their purpose was eventually forgotten."

"What happened with the observations of the North celestial pole?" I asked.

"Those continued for some time, but it soon became apparent to the observers that the North celestial pole had returned to its accustomed location and moved in the same slow orbit around Ptah as before. The conclusion was inescapable: the Earth had been heavily damaged by the Flood, and its alignment and movements disrupted by the catastrophe. But order had returned. The measurements from the Meidum pyramid and the Shining Pyramids of Dashur had confirmed this."

It was difficult for me to believe that the ancient Egyptians would go to all the trouble of modifying and erecting such huge structures as the Meidum and Dashur pyramids for so little information, none of it seemingly that practical. But the memory of the Flood catastrophe must have remained very much alive in their minds and the knowledge that the pyramids gave them clearly made the effort worthwhile.

I stared at the space between the Bent Pyramid and the small pyramid on its south side. I could easily imagine the ancient priests standing where I stood and looking up at the night sky, their attention drawn to the tip of the white arrow created by the fire between the two pyramids as it reflected off the face of the smaller one and onto the face of the upper part of the larger. I admired the skill it took to design and build such marvelous structures, and to use them to conduct the long and careful observations of the heavens over many long years.

Hordadef interrupted my thoughts. "It is time for us to go. We need to go to Saqqara and it is getting late. Besides, we need to stop for lunch soon. I haven't eaten anything at all today and I'm hungry."

"Let's go then," I said.

On our way out of the desert, I thought once again what an extremely interesting morning it had been.

11

Khufu

Khufu was the second Pharaoh of the 4th Dynasty. The Greeks called him Cheops, the name that he is widely and popularly known by. The building of the Pyramid has long been attributed to his efforts, as it was in ancient times. Little information regarding his life or reign survives and even that may be no more than hearsay. There remains no decent painting or statue of him. Were it not for the Pyramid, his name would have long since passed into obscurity. The Pyramid sustains his memory and marks his place in history.

As we drove up the road from Dashur to Saqqara, I voiced some of these thoughts. "Hordadef, if the Pyramid was built before the Flood, why is its construction almost universally attributed to Khufu?" To me this seemed the strongest argument against the countervailing theory of its Flood connection. And, although Khufu's connection to the Pyramid was mostly the stuff of legend, why couldn't it be true? Hordadef, true to form, was quick and confident in his responses.

"It is true that Khufu's name has been and will forevermore be associated with the Pyramid because of his labors on it. But we need to understand the nature of his connection to it, as it not only provides the answer that we are immediately looking for but helps to explain why his reputation has suffered so afterward. Simply stated, Khufu repaired the extensive damage that the Pyramid had suffered during the Flood and its aftermath. If this had been his only involvement with it, then he would likely have been remembered as a just and benevolent king. But he chose to usurp the noble structure as his own and to use its surrounding areas as a burial plot for his family and friends. This is what earned him great enmity among the people, and for this his memory has been held in disrepute ever since.

"Khufu's family was descended from merchants and cattle ranchers in the Delta region, who had grown fabulously wealthy on their ventures. They traded Egypt's manufactured goods, including clothing, jewelry, leather goods, and stoneware, for wines, oils, and timber from their trading partners throughout the Eastern Mediterranean region. The family was also prominent in Egypt's ruling circles and had intermarried with the ruling family for several generations. When Huni, the last Pharaoh of the 3rd Dynasty, died, he left no male heir, and so the throne passed to Sneferu, Khufu's father, by virtue of his marriage to a royal princess and with the approval of the royal family. Sneferu was a young man when he ascended the throne and he enjoyed a long and prosperous reign.

"Khufu would not have inherited the throne had his three older brothers not died prematurely. But when Sneferu died, his father's ministers and the royal family conferred and agreed that Khufu would become king, even though he was still little more than a boy. The older members of the government and his family agreed to watch over him and ensure that his actions were informed and tempered until he became old enough and mature enough to rule unassisted. Above all else they craved stability in their personal affairs and in the affairs of state, so an orderly transition of power to the new king was in everyone's best interest, even if the new king was little more than just a child.

"Most prominent in this respect was Hemon, Sneferu's brother and Vizier, the most powerful man in the government and in the palace. It was Hemon who negotiated and then backed a decision to make Khufu the king and it was primarily he who acted as regent during the new king's minority, although Sneferu's great queen, Khufu's mother, still exerted considerable influence over the affairs of the palace and remained a power to be reckoned with.

"Khufu proved an able and energetic king, but his reign was not without problems. He married Merytyetes, a blond-haired, green-eyed woman of European descent whose family had long traded and intermarried with Sneferu's family. Merytyetes was beautiful, charming, and intelligent, but she was not a native Egyptian—which would spawn several highly contentious and dangerous palace intrigues and conspiracies. Hemon was aware of the resentment that some in the extended royal family harbored toward Merytyetes. He attempted to resolve this by having Khufu take a native Egyptian as a second wife. The choice was Henutsen, a royal princess and every inch a worthy rival for Merytyetes in beauty, charm, and intellect. Henutsen, however, was also ambitious, and because of this there would never be true peace between the families of the two women. Eventually their rivalry led to bloodshed, but that was a long way off.

"Sneferu's reign was dominated by three great projects, all related to one another: repair and refurbish the ancient monuments and astronomical observatories; confirm the location and movement of the North celestial pole;

and resolve the great controversy that Imhotep had initiated with his claim that the Earth rotated on its axis and orbited the Sun. All three had been started before his reign and his predecessors had dedicated much time and effort to them, but considerable work remained when he ascended the throne.

"He was determined to complete all three in his lifetime but, with the possible exception of the second, did not achieve this goal. The first could not be completed as long as the controversy surrounding Imhotep's theory raged on, which led to increasingly bitter fighting between the opposing priestly factions. The ancient structures were modified and then modified again, all in a largely futile effort to resolve the long-smoldering and dangerous debate.

"Imhotep's supporters became known as the partisans of Ptah, while those who retained the orthodox beliefs became known as the partisans of Atum Re. There was a religious basis for the dispute. If Imhotep were correct, then Ptah, sitting on the Great Seat, would have to be the most important divine mechanism of the universe instead of the Sun. The partisans of Atum Re, of course, took the contrary position and believed that the Sun was the principal divine mechanism of the universe. Religious principles aside, however, the real reason for the rancor was the fight over the prestige and patronage from the royal palace that would most likely accrue to the temple of the victors. This drove the dispute even after it became clear that Imhotep's theory was correct. Unfortunately, the priestly controversy could not be contained and spilled over into palace politics, which eventually led to tragedy.

"Sneferu had believed that proof for or against Imhotep's theory would resolve the controversy and poured the resources of the land into the pyramid projects. Khufu had other ambitions. He set his sights on the greatest structure of all, the Great Pyramid, and was determined to complete its reconstruction in his lifetime. There was no room for competing projects or distractions of any sort if he was to succeed at this, and he knew it. When Khufu halted the projects at Dashur and Meidum and accepted Imhotep's theories the partisans of Ptah were elated, but the disappointment and sense of betrayal in the opposing camp was keenly felt and they began plotting to reverse their fortunes.

"Many court officials and members of the royal family supported the partisans of Ptah, more from their own beliefs than any rivalry with the opposing camp. Merytyetes and her family were committed to the partisans of Ptah, while Henutsen and her family, who seemed indifferent to the controversy, were secretly committed to the partisans of Atum Re. The families fed on one another's resentment and anger, while patiently biding their time until an opportunity presented itself for them to exact their vengeance.

"Khufu was largely unaware of the dark and sinister currents that flowed beneath the outwardly tranquil surface of the royal palace. But his ministers, particularly Hemon, had their spies in the palace and were well aware of what was afoot. It was too dangerous to move against Henutsen and her family, not only because of their alliances with the partisans of Atum Re, but also because they had many powerful and prominent relatives in Upper Egypt. Such action could result in far-reaching repercussions throughout the land. Better to monitor and keep abreast of the situation rather than risk precipitating unwanted and dangerous conflict.

"The project to repair the Great Pyramid had been under consideration for a number of years, and substantial planning had already gone into it. It proved a much larger project than anyone could have imagined, one that would severely tax the manpower and material resources of the entire kingdom. But as long as the great controversy between the partisans of Ptah and those of Atum Re raged on, and essential resources were being consumed in the struggle, there was no possibility of starting it. This was Khufu's principal reason for attempting to resolve the controversy as quickly as possible, regardless of his beliefs. He then immediately turned his attentions to the Pyramid, confident that his decision would be accepted as the final word on the matter. However, if he thought that the great controversy could be ended simply by royal decree, he and his counselors, especially Hemon, were sadly mistaken.

"The first part of the project involved removing the immense piles of debris and broken stones that had fallen away from the structure and encumbered it on all four sides. Simultaneously, the structure was thoroughly surveyed to ascertain the extent of the damage and to begin devising plans for making repairs. This survey also involved removing significant amounts of intact stone in order to investigate the nature and extent of any damage that the interior structures may have sustained. All of the Pyramid's chambers were entered and thoroughly examined. If there were ever any items of value in the Pyramid, they most assuredly were removed at this time.

"Once these preliminary steps were completed, the reconstruction began in earnest. The great canal that had been used to help build the Pyramid was repaired and placed back into service. This part of the project alone took almost 10 years to complete. But with a working canal, the repair crews could move the large quantities of stone and materials that were needed. Without it the project would have been almost impossible.

"As revealed by the survey, the damage of most concern to Khufu's architects and stonemasons was the long crack in the granite ceiling of the King's Chamber, along the south wall, probably caused by the severe earthquakes during the great Flood. Their concern was not so much for the ceiling crack, bad as it was, but for the integrity of the hidden structures above the King's Chamber, which formed the *djed* column. There was no way of knowing whether they were damaged as well, and if they were, to what extent. If the damage was severe and these structures had collapsed, they had to be repaired or it could jeopardize the other chambers in the Pyramid and possibly its exterior as well.

"Initially the architects thought about cutting around the structures from below, but this was considered too dangerous. If they were damaged, it could precipitate further collapse and damage. This could also jeopardize the lives of the stonemasons. They had no choice: the upper tiers of the Pyramid would have to be partially dismantled to allow for a more thorough assessment of the hidden structures. This was a time-consuming approach, to be certain, but those responsible wanted it done right. Repairing the main structure was impossible until any damage to the interior structures was thoroughly assessed and repaired as necessary. The assessment took several years, but when it was completed they found the internal structures intact. The crack in the ceiling of the King's Chamber apparently was an isolated matter. The repairs to the main structure could now proceed.

"Once the repair project was initiated, it quickly became apparent to all concerned that it would be an enormous undertaking and would seriously tax Egypt's resources for decades to come. Labor, repair materials, boats, skilled craftsmen, and a vast staff of scribes and overseers to supervise and file reports on the project's progress were all in great demand. At first the project received the unquestioning support of the *nomes*, or provinces, and the towns and cities of the land. But soon this support waned as the demands of the project continued relentlessly and in fact grew with the passing of time.

"Khufu managed to maintain support for the project without serious disruption for a number of years. But as it dragged on, support among officials from those areas beyond Memphis dwindled until he was subjected to more and more vocal and brazen challenges. His own influence ebbing, he turned to his sons and daughters, particularly Prince Kawab and Princess Hetepheres, to serve as emissaries to keep provincial officials behind the project. This worked for a while. Princess Hetepheres, who possessed great beauty and charm, was particularly effective. But even her influence faded as the project dragged on and on, with no firm end in sight.

"The provincials were right to complain. So much of their local labor and material resources flowed to the capital to support the project that they were forced to curtail all local building projects and close their temples for lack of means to support them. This further aggravated the situation by alienating the local population, placing further pressure on the provincial officials. Pressure for change quickly built and soon found an outlet. When it did come it manifested itself not only in the kingdom but in the king's own household, where it was the most serious.

"Politics are an ever-present fact of life in a royal palace and Khufu's was no exception. The existing and growing struggles between the factions of the great Queens, Merytyetes and Henutsen, for prestige and prominence in the royal palace provided a natural stage for giving expression to the larger disputes in the kingdom. The great controversy and its religious quarrels that had been inspired by Imhotep's theories had already divided the priestly cast and spilled over into palace politics. This alone most likely would not have dangerously destabilized the palace, but for the dispute over the demands and costs of the Pyramid project entering the fray. The weight of their combined impact was tragic. Blood soon flowed as familial disputes and rivalries within the royal family rapidly escalated beyond the ability of palace officials to control them.

"Prince Kawab, Khufu's eldest son by Merytyetes, was heir to the throne. A talented young man, he grew more and more active in the affairs of government while his father focused his attention almost exclusively on the Pyramid project. Kawab had shown himself to be an able administrator, but he was too inexperienced to fully appreciate the dangers surrounding him in the palace from the factional disputes. The palace chamberlain, who ordinarily monitored and controlled such disputes, was old and had grown inept. He was either not aware of the depths of the enmity that existed between the two factions or indifferent to it. In any case, it proved fatal to him.

"No one can say exactly how it happened, but Kawab and the chamberlain were both killed instantly when a brick wall collapsed on them as they strolled about the palace gardens, apparently engaged in conversation. An investigation revealed that the wall might have been intentionally undermined, allowing it to be brought down with ease, but failed to prove these suspicions or to reveal who might have been responsible.

"Word of the deaths spread rapidly and rumors arose that the two men had been intentionally assassinated on the orders of Khufu, who supposedly learned that they were conspiring to curtail any further work on the Pyramid. This news sparked an already volatile atmosphere in Memphis and in several restless provinces that had been building for a long time. Violent riots erupted in a number of areas throughout the land. The army was called out and immediately subdued the riots, but not without terrible bloodshed and destruction of property. When the flames of chaos finally died down, the battle lines between the Merytyetes and Henutsen factions were radically altered. Baufre, Merytyetes's youngest son and little more than a child, became Crown Prince, while Henutsen had succeeded in placing her brother in the chamberlain's position. Khufu was crushed by the death of Kawab but was determined more than ever to finish the Pyramid, which was finally nearing completion. Great celebrations were planned to commemorate the event, but it was overshadowed by additional bloodshed in the palace.

"Not long after the Pyramid was completed, Baufre sickened and quickly died while on a visit to a remote town in the Delta. Suspicion fell on a cook, but before the investigation could proceed he took his own life, or so it seemed. News of this added tragedy was too much for the old king and he died not long after, a crushed and broken man. He had completed his lifelong project but it brought him little joy, so great was his sadness over the deaths of his two sons.

"After Khufu's funeral, the Merytyetes and Henutsen factions met and agreed that Djedefre, a son of Khufu by a minor Queen, would marry Princess Hetepheres, daughter of Merytyetes, and become Pharaoh. It was further agreed by the two sides that Khafre, Henutsen's son, would become Crown Prince. Neither faction was enamored of the arrangements, but they did restore a sense of calm and order to a chaotic situation that could have brought down the entire dynasty if not brought under control. Relative peace descended over the palace. But it did not last.

"Several years after Djedefre ascended the throne he too died under suspicious circumstances, but by then Henutsen was determined to finish the clash with Merytyetes and dispose of her rival and family once and for all. Merytyetes and Hetepheres were banished to temples in Upper Egypt, while their remaining family members and supporters were turned out of the palace and relegated to minor roles in government. Khafre was crowned Pharaoh and the priests of Atum Re, long opposed to Khufu because of his summary acceptance of Imhotep's theories and the great patronage he had lavished on the Temple of Ptah and its priests, were quickly rewarded for their longstanding support for Queen Henutsen in her contest with Queen Merytyetes and her family. A number of them were placed in prestigious positions within the new government and vastly increased patronage soon flowed to the Temple of Atum Re and its priests. Imhotep's theories were not denounced. They were simply ignored and soon forgotten, at least by the vast majority of priests.

"A great era had come to an end, though few probably recognized it at the time. The reigns of Khufu and his father, Sneferu, had not been without controversy and civic unrest, but they had both witnessed an expansion of knowledge among the greatest in history. Their reigns saw the final struggles of a rebirth of civilization, which was once so much in doubt after the Great Flood. And in a very real sense the restoration of the Pyramid was the culmination of this long process. Egypt would go on to flourish for thousands of years, and the fruits of civilization that she had once protected and nurtured and worried over in the aftermath of the Flood would eventually grow strong and then spread far and wide. The Pyramid would become the defining symbol of this great era, and its restoration the final step in the triumph of order over the chaos of the Flood.

"And what of Khufu, you might ask? Where lies his grave? He may have been buried in the King's Chamber of the Pyramid. Or he may have been buried elsewhere in the vicinity of the Pyramid. No one can say for certain now. But in the final analysis, what does it matter? While his name will forever be associated with the Pyramid, neither did he conceive of it nor did he build it. Its purpose was far greater than to serve as a mere tomb for a mortal king of men, and Khufu must have been aware of this fact. He did, however, labor mightily on it and he did fully commit the resources of a young Egyptian civilization to restoring it. History has maligned him for it ever since, and in many respects properly so for turning the Pyramid's immediate vicinity into a private burial plot for his friends and family members. But if this was truly his greatest sin, then should we not forgive him such vanity in light of his great achievement? Is not the Pyramid much greater than any of this, and did not Khufu honor its true meaning by restoring it?"

"Yes," I said. "History seems to have been unfair to him."

Hordadef paused, only for a moment. "Do you know where the name 'Khufu' comes from, Mr. Richard?"

"I have no idea. I've never heard an explanation or learned anything of its source."

"It comes from the Pyramid itself and embodies its great cosmic significance."

He took out a small notebook and pen. First he drew the hieroglyphs for Khufu's name (Figure #25), for the kh sound in his name and a more elaborate rendering of the hieroglyph for the f sound. He said that the second version was an acceptable alternative rendering of Khufu's name as the ancient Egyptians rarely used vowels in their writing.

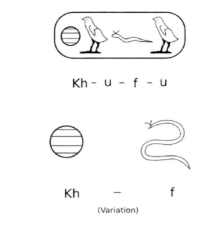

Kh - u - f - u

Kh   —   f

(Variation)

Terrestrial globe with axis
of ecliptic and Ptah
in the Heart-of-the-Dragon
(Constellation of Draco)

Variation with symbol
for *Wepwawet*, the
Opener-of-Ways.

∨   ⌒
Wep   -   t

Khufu's Name

Figure 25

Next he drew a line between the *kh* and *f* that terminated in a small cross near the center of the second hieroglyph. This line was the axis of the ecliptic and the cross marked the location of Ptah, the Great Seat. He added two more hieroglyphs that he said spelled the word *wepwawet,* or Opener of Ways, a common epithet for Osiris.

"So you see, Mr. Richard, Khufu's name arises from the Osiris structures in the Pyramid, which in turn generate the terrestrial sphere that is connected to Ptah through the axis of the ecliptic. Impressive, is it not?

"Very much so, but you still haven't told me what it means."

"What it means? Mr. Richard, there are some things that are beyond meaning and this is one of them. There is no doubt that the symbols embodied in Khufu's name are of profound cosmological significance, but their meaning is something beyond man's grasp and known only to God."

I continued to stare at the drawing but did not reply.

"I have one final thing to say regarding Khufu and the people of his time that I have referred to in my story. They no longer have voices to speak for themselves. And if I have spoken wrongly of them and harmed their memory, then I humbly apologize to them and beg God's forgiveness for this transgression. For in the end, only He knows the actions of men and what lies in their hearts, and only He may judge them."

12

Saqqara

Saqqara. The desert realm of Sokar. He who sits on his throne in his chamber beneath the Earth, which not even the Sun god can penetrate. He who receives the falcon, the dweller who lives in beams of light and carries the fire of heaven that is the source of creation. He of the outstretched wings in the living egg of light. Sokar. Lord of resurrection and rebirth.

Saqqara has always been a place of fascination and wonder to me. It is the site of the Step Pyramid, without doubt one of the most significant stone structures ever built by human hand, and one of the oldest. It was used as a burial ground from the beginning of, and throughout, Egypt's long history. Walking around the site and contemplating its ancient past, one gets the sense that countless generations have done the same over the ages, and that the shadows over the land are deep and long and hide many secrets. For every secret recovered from the sand, another has been rendered that much more obscure under the spoil of excavation. Still, it is the Step Pyramid that draws the eye and gives the site its focus.

I was delighted that Hordadef wanted to visit there, but as much as I enjoyed going, his interest in the site and its relevance to our discussions was hard for me to understand. But he had so often surprised and shocked me when I expressed similar doubts, I knew from experience to keep my silence and just listen. Whatever the purpose, I was thrilled to be there.

As we crested the desert hill beyond the vegetation of the village of Saqqara, the first site our eyes beheld was the Step Pyramid. It looked majestic against the late afternoon Sun. After we parked the car and started walking toward it, Hordadef suddenly stopped.

"No. It is impolite not to pay our respects to the dead first."

And so, after paying our entry and parking fees, we headed off into the desert north of the pyramid. Within several hundred feet we were alone and silence closed in around us. Almost everywhere we stepped were pieces of mud brick or broken pottery. The area seemed covered with them. Now and then we encountered what looked like bits of bone, but maybe I was imagining that. In any case, it gave me the impression that we were quite literally walking on the past.

We headed for a rise to the east that obscured the vegetation of the Nile Valley beyond. Hordadef stopped. When I questioned him, in a hoarse whisper he forcefully told me to be quiet. He pointed to what resembled a small dog scurrying off toward a series of small caves in the sand.

"There he is," he said, smiling broadly. "Saqqara's true guardian: the jackal."

It was a thrilling sight. I had never seen one, and would have thought them extinct in such places. But there it was, running across the desert as its ancestors had done since time immemorial. As I followed it with my eyes, Hordadef declared, "He has acknowledged our presence and granted us permission to be here. Now we can proceed about our business." His statement seemed quite appropriate to the circumstances, and the jackal's presence more certain permission than the passes we had just purchased.

We turned and headed back to the Step Pyramid. As we neared the entryway past the ancient walls that surrounded it, Hordadef asked, "Mr. Richard, do you know what first brought men to this place?"

I told him everything I knew about Sokar and the area's use as a burial ground.

"Very good. It seems you learned quite a bit more in that university of yours than I had imagined. But you did not answer my question. What first attracted men here?"

"I guess because it was near the city of Memphis, and they needed a prominent area to bury their dead."

"What if I told you that the reason this place was chosen as the site for the many monuments that are here was no more a matter of random choice than was the choice for the site of the Pyramid? What if I told you that this precise spot was chosen for a specific reason?"

"If that's the answer you're looking for, I can't tell you what it is. I don't know."

Hordadef led me into the great courtyard that lies in front of the pyramid. "The Step Pyramid covers one of the most sacred sites in all the land, or at least the site was once among the most sacred. But even after it lost its religious significance, for thousands of years it continued to attract men, who remembered that their ancestors had considered it sacred. But the reason men first came here, Mr. Richard, is the Moon. It made its northernmost approach here in its orbits about the Earth, before returning south, in an 18.6-year cycle that defined the limits of its orbital movements within the Band of the Ecliptic. Here, Mr. Richard, was the Moon's equivalent to the Sun's Tropic of Cancer, and its northern tropic or turning point. But the Moon's movements are not as regular as the Earth's, and this eventually resulted in a shift of this line toward the south, some 70 to 80 miles away, where it lies today. When this happened I cannot say, but when it did Saqqara lost its original sacred meaning."

"So the Step Pyramid was used to observe the passage of the Moon at its turning point in the heavens?"

"Not exactly. By the time the Step Pyramid was built, after several structures had preceded it on this spot, the turning point of the Moon had long since shifted south. The original shrine that marked the Moon's turning was built deep underground, at the bottom of a great shaft cut into the rock, in a square chamber. Four corridors led away from it toward the four cardinal points—north, south, east, and west—and a number of additional corridors and side chambers ran from each of these.

"The shrine itself was rectangular with walls of alabaster, a floor of diorite, and a ceiling of limestone beams that had five-pointed stars carved into their undersides, all finely finished and closely set. The ceiling had a round hole cut into it that could be closed off with a stone stopper, specially designed for the purpose. Above the shrine was a great wooden beam, held aloft on massive supports and fitted with ropes that could be used to raise the stone plug and swing it out of the way, and to lower it back into position. This upper part of the shrine could not be seen from the surrounding passages and chambers.

"Now, inside the chamber was a large, thimble-shaped block of limestone plated with gold. It sat directly in the center of the shrine but could not be seen from the outside, due to the opacity of the alabaster. This object was the Egg of Sokar.

"On the ground level above, the area surrounding the shaft was enclosed by a large, square, stone *mastaba*, which was finished with finely carved Tura limestone. On the platform of the *mastaba*, the opening of the shaft was closed off by large wooden beams, which in turn were covered over with a smooth layer of small limestone blocks and plaster. The shaft cover was designed to be removed and replaced as needed.

"Once every 18.6 years, when the Moon rose high enough in the heavens to approach its northern turning point, the priests marked its precise progress with the east-west sighting passageway of stone columns that lies immediately inside the entryway through the surrounding walls of the pyramid complex. Using this mechanism the priests could determine the precise date when the Moon would reach its turning point over the sacred chamber. If it was going to reach full phase at the same time, the priests alerted their colleagues and the palace to the approaching occasion. But if the Moon was not expected to reach full phase at its turning point during the season in which the occasion was celebrated, no formal ceremonies of the observation were held and the next celebration would await the passing of another 18.6 years.

"If all of the conditions were right and the Moon full, they removed the cover from the shaft above the shrine and lifted and removed the stopper from the shrine's ceiling. Then they inspected and cleaned the maze of passageways and chambers surrounding the subterranean shrine.

"On the day of this singular occasion, a great feast of food and wine was held after sunset in the courtyard in front of the shaft. Afterward, guests were directed down the long, narrow stairway that led under the *mastaba* to the corridors surrounding the shrine. Priests positioned along the way guided them in the pitch-black darkness. They waited in silence until the approach of the great moment, when the priests signaled the celebrants to gather near the chamber of the shrine. As they stood before it, a faint light began to glow within, and grew larger and brighter by the minute.

"As the celebrants watched, the light assumed the shape of two outstretched wings, held open by a figure of light. The movement of the image's soft light along the alabaster walls was mesmerizing. No matter from which aspect the dazzling display was observed, its appearance was the same. The moment of the great visitation had arrived. It was one of those truly magical displays that the ancient Egyptian priests were so capable of: at once powerfully dramatic, filled with the most profound of meanings, and serenely beautiful. A true wonder, more so when its sacred significance is understood.

"The ancient Egyptians believed that every evening the Sun set and descended below the western horizon to a dark and endless cavern, where it was rejuvenated and its light renewed for the coming day. This cavern was also the abode of the dead and the place where Osiris lay after his body was recovered and hidden in the Earth by his sisters, Isis and Nephthys. It was the land of shadow. Before the Sun entered this cavern, its remaining light was entrusted to the Moon. When the Moon passed over the depths of the cavern, its light parted the shadows, where it found the darkened Sun and restored its light. The Sun was then reborn as it began its ascent once more into the heavens. They believed that all life was renewed in this same way. This was the moment Sokar was said to stir in his egg of light; the moment of rebirth and resurrection. The shrine in Saqqara was designed to celebrate this moment with its dramatic display in the darkened depths of the Earth at night."

When Hordadef paused I took the opportunity to ask, "What happened to the shrine? I've never read or heard anything about it."

"Once the priests observed that the Moon had permanently altered its path in the heavens, the shrine no longer functioned and lost its purpose. But the people still remembered the ancient ceremonies and considered the site sacred. So the priests decided to transform the site, making it a memorial to the primeval mound that was said to have emerged from the depths of the abyss when the Earth was created, after the very first time the light stirred in Sokar's Egg. This is the meaning of the Step Pyramid: it is the primeval mound that arose at the beginning of time, and the Earth reborn after the Flood.

"Before the pyramid was built, however, the alabaster and diorite shrine was broken up and used for packing blocks around the granite mausoleum, which now lies at the bottom of the shaft and was used as a grave for the Pharaoh Zoser. The pyramid was built during his reign and its architect was Imhotep, the Greatest of Seers."

"All of this is very interesting," I said, "but what does it have to do with the Pyramid and the Flood?"

"The Pyramid. Yes, of course. It is good that you remind me. The shrine of Sokar was built before the Flood and was one of Egypt's most sacred sites. When it was determined that the Earth would suffer a grievous blow from the heavens, threatening all life, some of the people came here and hid food, water, and the things they would need to restart their lives, if they survived. They hid these things in the depths of the Earth, in the widespread maze of tunnels and passageways carved under this whole area, which run for considerable distances in almost every direction."

"But why here? Why did they come to this place?"

"It was sacred to them because it celebrated the rebirth of life. It offered them hope when death stalked them. There was no more fitting place for them to come. So they brought their families and friends here. At the approach of the terrible goddess, they said their farewells to one another, prayed for God's mercy, and awaited their fate."

"Did the people themselves go underground for shelter?"

"Who can say? Some may have, but these underground tunnels could have been their graves if they flooded, which was a real possibility. I believe that most of them stayed above the ground and sought such shelter as they could find against the chaos that arose all around them.

"The memories of the shrine at Saqqara and its use as a place of vigil and sanctuary during the Flood catastrophe permeated many later myths, particularly those surrounding Osiris and his resurrection from the dead. People eventually forgot the specific details of what went on here, but they remembered that it was sacred ground. Egypt continued to bring its dead here for countless generations because it was the land of rebirth, resurrection, and life everlasting. These things would never be forgotten. Until the shrine was closed, people came here yearly for a feast in honor of Sokar and rebirth. Large quantities of food and dishes were stored in the underground passages and chambers. But when the shrine was closed, all of this ended."

"Did the people who sought refuge here during the Flood survive it?"

"Some must have. Otherwise there would have been no one in the Land of Egypt after that. But those who survived lived to see a world utterly destroyed and forever changed. No doubt many felt they would have been better off dying than surviving and suffering such privation. A few, though, believed that one day Earth would recover. They struggled to keep the ancient memories alive for that eventual rebirth."

"Were there other places of refuge in Egypt that were used during the Flood?"

"I'm sure there were, but I don't know where."

Hordadef and I gazed silently at the extensive ruins all around. Even in their present condition they were impressive, especially the Step Pyramid. He lit a cigarette. I could only wonder how many of his ancestors had come to this same spot to look upon this same scene. I got the identical feeling about him here that I had gotten at the Pyramid. He belonged here and in his own way he was just as timeless as the ancient structures around us. Perhaps more so, as he had the ability to make them viable again and restore to them their ancient meaning.

"Come, Mr. Richard. It is growing dark and there is one other sight here that I want to show you." He tamped out the cigarette on the heel of his shoe and put it in his pocket. As he did so, he looked at me. "Are you ready?"

"You lead and I'll follow."

With that we set off quickly along the pyramid's eastern face until we arrived at its northern face. Then we made our way around a series of ruins, eventually arriving at a small structure at the base of the northern face.

"Come close and look," Hordadef said, motioning me forward.

I looked into what could have been a set of stone binoculars if they had had lenses in the eyepieces. At the other end was a small chamber where a statue of Pharaoh Zoser sat, staring through the stone binoculars at the northern sky. The statue was mounted on a slightly inclined surface so that its gaze was permanently lifted to the heavens.

"It's the same statue of Zoser that we saw back in the Cairo Museum, except it's a replica," I said.

"You'll notice that his eyes have been gouged out. Do you know why?"

"I guess someone wanted to destroy Zoser's memory."

"Possibly, but more likely they wanted them because they were made of carefully cut crystals that made one feel the statue could actually see, which made it lifelike. You asked me when we first met if the Pyramid contained any malleable glass, as the legends you spoke of claimed. All I can tell you is that there may have been, but it was probably made of crystal like Zoser's eyes and most likely was removed long ago. The crystals were considered unique and valuable, as no one alive could recall how they were made or what tools were used to craft them. All they knew was that in the distant past someone knew how to cut and shape the crystals, but the art had been lost over the years. Anyhow, that is my answer to your question. I also wanted you to see Zoser's statue in its intended setting. Would you not agree that the image of Zoser is seated and looking up at the heavens?"

"Yes, but with his eyes missing he appears blind to whatever he's looking at."

"And that is precisely what I wanted you to see. Zoser and the learned men of his age, such as Imhotep, watched the heavens almost incessantly to learn heaven's order and, as best they were able, to understand it. In this respect they were no different than people who watch the heavens today. The ancients, however, grasped the larger meaning and purpose of what they saw and were ever mindful of its Creator and in awe of His great acts. Nowadays the watchers are more like this statue of Zoser with its eyes gouged out—blind because they forget that which should never be forgotten. They look, they have knowledge, but they have no real understanding of what it is they are looking at.

"It grows dark. The Antiquities guards will be looking for us, so we should go."

We made our way back through the tangle of ruins to the courtyard and then out through the gate in the walls to the parking lot, where our car sat alone. Darkness had set in and the Moon was rising to the southeast. It was almost full and quite spectacular. I tried to imagine what the ancient priests must have thought when they watched it rise. Truly they must have been awed in its presence, and lost in wonder as to how and why it came to be and of its meaning in the Divine Order of Heaven. If Hordadef was right and modern man has forgotten these things, they have indeed become blind men who look but do not see, and we are all the lesser for it.

13

Plea of the Ages

I awoke late. My time in Egypt was almost at an end. My return flight left in the predawn hours of the following day.

On the way back to the hotel from Saqqara, Hordadef and I had agreed that he would take me to the airport. We settled our financial arrangements, but truth be told what he had given me was priceless. There was no way I could properly compensate him for it. Knowledge of the ages for a mere pittance! Over the course of our time together I had come to realize what he undoubtedly already understood: money was merely a device for him to focus my attention and to establish an outward appearance of formality and purpose to our relationship. I was his pupil and he was my teacher. Our relationship was really founded on trust, not money. He taught me what he knew because I was willing to learn, and through the fits and starts of our relationship he understood this probably better than I did myself. In the final analysis, I can only properly pay him by honoring the priceless legacy that he entrusted to me.

He said he had one final lesson for me and that it would be most fitting to give it on the plateau at sunset. We agreed to meet in the same spot in front of the Pyramid where I had had my first lesson. How appropriate! I had no idea what it might involve, as I thought there was no more to be said on the subject. But Hordadef was a man of surprises and had never once disappointed me. So I anticipated it with great interest.

I spent the afternoon lounging around the pool, engaging in idle chatter with other tourists. But mostly I reflected on all that I had learned. Hordadef had told me so much that, even though I had taken notes, it would take a while to fully understand it all. The more that I thought about it the more my admiration for him grew. The depth and breadth of his knowledge was staggering. I'm certain he'd brought it all down to my level of understanding as best he could. I also thought about the improbability of my quest and how it had all turned out. But mostly what I thought about were the legends of the Pyramid that had preoccupied me for so long and had brought me here.

I found everything that I had been looking for. The legends of the Arabs and Jews were not fanciful stories but had all proven true. The majority of them, anyway. The terrestrial globe, celestial spheres, knowledge of geometry and physics, star charts—they were all in the Pyramid, just as the legends had said. And the records of that singular catastrophe, the Flood—they too were there. What's more, I had found their source: the Egyptians who had both built the Pyramid and later passed along the knowledge of its purpose and significance. They were the source. Much of the knowledge in the Pyramid was carried over into the religion and myths of the later dynastic Egyptians, where it lived on for thousands of years. It was all there, as it had been right from the start, which raised a number of questions. How had we managed to lose sight of some of the most significant events in human history? If the Pyramid is a monument to the eternal order that exists between Heaven and Earth, how and why did we forget that?

These profoundly disturbing questions were best left to others to ponder, but inevitably the only conclusion possible was our inherent mortal weakness. And therein lay the second reason for the Pyramid, and by far the more important of the two. (The first being, of course, to preserve this knowledge from the Flood catastrophe.) The Pyramid was built to withstand the ravages of man's ignorance and folly, and to preserve those things that should never be forgotten. The perils of the Flood were of little consequence compared to these threats. Over time human beings grow arrogant, condescending, and contemptuous toward all things that lie beyond our knowledge or control. These are fatal errors. The order that exists between Heaven and Earth also extends to our souls and therein lay the ultimate lesson in all of this. Human beings are but a part of creation, and we are bound to its Divine Order in ways that we can never fully comprehend and for reasons that will forever remain a mystery to us. The Pyramid is there to remind us of these things. It is our responsibility to heed its message and to learn to live our lives in accordance with God's Order.

The Pyramid is a relic from another time, a distant age that exists now only in myth and legend. It is a profoundly moving testament to all that its people believed and held sacred. Knowing that death and destruction were about to overwhelm them and that the Earth itself might perish, they selected those precious few things that they believed most worth preserving and bequeathing to their descendants. What they chose to memorialize in its stones was their unswerving faith in the Divine Order of the universe, the order that God had founded at the act of creation and that our very existence depends upon. Faced with certain death, the architects of the Pyramid set aside their pettiness and selfishness, lifted their eyes to Heaven, and spoke of these things to the ages. If there is greatness and majesty in the Pyramid, this is its source. This makes it truly awe-inspiring.

Such were my thoughts as I awaited the sunset hour. From the mundane to the sublime and back again. But there was more. Everything about my trip had a dreamlike feel to it—my quest, Egypt, the Pyramid and the other ancient monuments, Hordadef. I felt like a member of an audience to a scripted play, except for the few insignificant bit parts I was assigned from time to time, with no knowledge of the plot or story line. Several times I wondered what I was even doing on the same stage as Hordadef. It was his play, not mine; he was the lead character, not me. For my part I walked around awkwardly, waited in the wings, sat in the audience—never certain what was expected of me but anxiously anticipating with great curiosity how it would all turn out.

And now I waited for the next scene to unfold. Soon enough the shadows lengthened as the appointed hour neared. I ate dinner, packed my things, and made the other necessary preparations for my trip home. I then left the hotel and started walking up the plateau for my last lesson with Hordadef. The Sun slipped below the horizon as I arrived at the top. The Pyramid was dark around its base, golden red around its mid section, and amber near the top, where it caught the Sun's final light. The stars had begun to show. A slight breeze was blowing.

I turned my attention to the parking lot and saw Hordadef leaning against his car, looking at me. He waved, and smiled broadly as I approached. I returned his wave and continued toward him.

"Ah, Mr. Richard. Good evening to you! What a beautiful night it is to conclude your visit to this beautiful and wondrous Land of Egypt, is it not?"

"It is indeed a very beautiful evening. I will hate to leave here."

"I trust that all is to your satisfaction with my stories?"

"Very much so. But I don't know how I can properly thank you for everything that you have taught me."

"Grow wise from it, Mr. Richard. Find wisdom. Honor this knowledge. Add to it as best you can. And in time, give it to others who might profit from it. That is my just and true compensation as a teacher, Mr. Richard.

"I told you earlier that I had one final lesson for you concerning the Pyramid, and so we will begin. Did you know that in addition to all the things I have shown you and told you, there is writing in the Pyramid as well?"

"No, I didn't!" This was a huge piece of news! I thought that any books or written material would have perished ages ago. Of all the things Hordadef had shown me, none of them looked like writing. "That would be very interesting to see. Are we going back into the Pyramid?"

"No, that won't be necessary," he said. "We can discuss it here. As you saw earlier, the 1st, 3rd, and 5th rows of blocks in the King's Chamber produce symbols, which can be combined with one another and interpreted in various ways. But they are also hieroglyphs, or sacred writing." He pulled a piece of paper from his pocket and drew the symbols for me again. "The meaning of the hieroglyph from the 1st row is Eternity. From the 2nd row, Heaven. And from the 3rd, Earth. In order, from bottom to top, they read 'Earth, Heaven, Eternity.' But the hieroglyphs when taken together also spell P-T-H, the word for Ptah, or God (Figure #26). As in all else with these symbols, there is a need for carefully considered interpretation and elaboration of the hieroglyphs in order to fully understand their meaning. In that sense I believe that no one properly calls upon God, except in prayer, which is what I believe was the authors' intent with these hieroglyphs. I understand them to be a plea to God that says, 'O Lord of Heaven and Earth, O Lord of Eternity, O God, hear our prayers.'

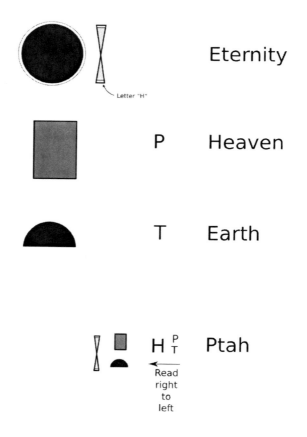

Hieroglyphic Messages in the Symbols of the 1st, 2nd and 3rd
Celestial Spheres
Figure 26

"Think of it, Mr. Richard. The Pyramid continuously calls upon God to hear our prayers and will do so for all eternity. In its form and shape, the Pyramid speaks to Him, calling on Him to see and know that humanity understands the Divine Order that binds Heaven and Earth. Is that not truly something to marvel at?"

"Yes, it is, Hordadef." I wanted to say more, but my mind raced at full speed in different directions. If this were true, the Pyramid was not mute after all, as countless generations had assumed, but spoke loudly and clearly the same message, over and over again through countless long ages. The ramifications of this lay well beyond proper contemplation for the time being. I could only shake my head in disbelief and wonder. It was stunning.

As we talked, I had barely taken notice that it had grown darker and darker, the hues from the sunset fading from the horizon. Hordadef turned suddenly and said, "Mr. Richard, look at the Pyramid."

The only thing that I could make out was its dark silhouette against the night sky. I finally admitted to him that I could hardly see it.

"Precisely!" he said. "God has taken it and hidden it away in shadow as he has done every night for thousands of years. Now look behind you at what the Pyramid gazes upon, Mr. Richard." As we turned, he directed my attention up to the stars in the heavens. "Look upon the glory of God's magnificent creation, Mr. Richard. Look at what He has wrought. It is truly a wonder, is it not?"

I had not anticipated this. His command surprised me. Nevertheless, I found myself awestruck by the stars and stood silently enthralled with their display for several long minutes, when I either recalled the words in my mind or Hordadef spoke them.

> *Do you not feel the stupendous power of the Earth as it moves in measured step to the Order set for it by the Hand of God at the beginning of time?*
>
> *And do you not see Earth's movements reflected in Heaven above, as cycles of time are endlessly repeated according to Divine Order for all eternity?*
>
> *And do you not know that time is but the shadow of God's presence in the universe, and that He is the Lord of Eternity, the Master of Time?*
>
> *Then do you not understand that the Pyramid stands between Heaven and Earth, and is a memorial to these things and a legacy to the ages?*

I was profoundly moved. I couldn't speak and stood humbled, staring up at the heavens. The only sound I could hear was the wind blowing, carrying off all my self-importance and pretense and stirring within me a sense of kinship and continuity with the universe that I had never known before. I will never forget that moment.

"Mr. Richard, it is time for you to go. Egypt is finished with you and you with her for the time being. But you are a part of this land now and it will always be with you. You will return one day soon, my friend, and then you and I will talk once more of the sacred things of Egypt. Until then, Mr. Richard, until then . . . ."

Appendix 1

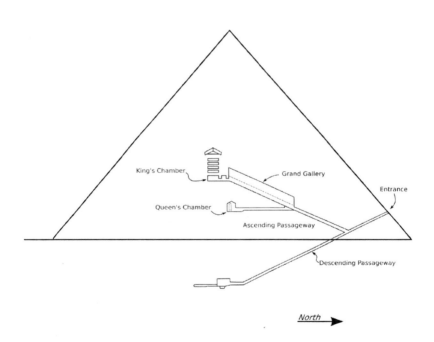

Interior Structures of the Great Pyramid

Appendix 2

Measurements Used to Generate
The Terrestrial Globe

Measurements and Their Survey Source:

1. Distance from the Pyramid's centerline to the center of the King's Chamber–**21 cubits** (Petrie)
2. Distance from the base of the Pyramid to the raised floor of the King's Chamber–**82.08 cubits** (Petrie)
3. Distance from the raised floor of the King's Chamber to the ceiling–**11.18 cubits** (Petrie)
4. Distance from the underside of the ceiling beams of the King's Chamber to the underside of the ceiling beams of the 4th superimposed chamber above it–**21.56 cubits** (Maragioglio & Rinaldi)
5. Distance from the base of the Pyramid to the bottom of the ceiling beams of the 4th superimposed chamber above the King's Chamber–**114.82 cubits** (Petrie and Maragioglio & Rinaldi)
6. Height of the Pyramid–**280 cubits**, including pyramidion (Petrie)
7. Height of the pyramidion –**2.06 cubits** (See Note 4 below)
8. Height of the Pyramid, excluding the pyramidion – **277.94 cubits** (Petrie and Note 4 below)
9. Base of the Pyramid–**440 cubits** (Petrie)

Notes:

1. Surveys cited were performed by 1) W.M. Flinders Petrie and 2) Maragioglio & Rinaldi.
2. All measurements are in Egyptian cubits. One Egyptian cubit equals 20.62 inches or 0.524 meters.
3. Margin of error factors, if any, were not used.
4. The measurement of the upper angle of the terrestrial sphere would be affected if the base of the pyramidion were used to swing the arc, instead of the peak of the capstone. The pyramidion was believed to be approximately 2.06 cubits high. (See Tompkins, Peter; *Secrets of the Great Pyramid*. New York. Harper and Row. 1971. Appendix by Livio Catullo Stecchini; *Notes on the Relation of Ancient Measures to the Great Pyramid*; pages 371-375, for a description of the pyramidion and the historical basis for its existence.)
5. The lower angle of the terrestrial sphere equates to the latitude reached by the leading edge of the rim of the Sun's disc at summer solstice. The midpoint of the Sun's disc would be 15 minutes lower in latitude and directly above the Tropic of Cancer at the summer solstice.

Appendix 3

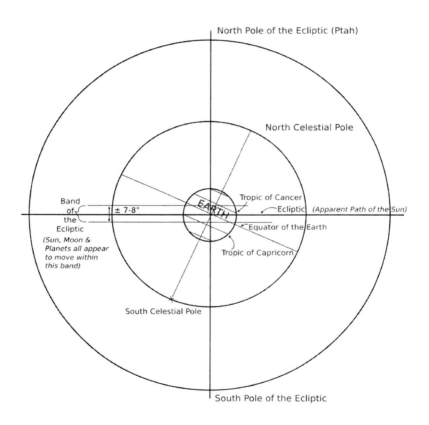

North Pole of the Ecliptic (Ptah)

North Celestial Pole

Band
of
the
Ecliptic
(Sun, Moon &
Planets all appear
to move within
this band)

± 7-8°

EARTH

Tropic of Cancer

Ecliptic *(Apparent Path of the Sun)*

Equator of the Earth

Tropic of Capricorn

South Celestial Pole

South Pole of the Ecliptic

Band of the Ecliptic

Printed in the United States
131196LV00006B/85-90/P

9 780595 490493